Tracking Jane, Episode 2

A Novella by
Eduardo Suastegui

Rover

Copyright © 2014, 2015, Eduardo Suastegui

Published by Eduardo Suastegui, Print edition, revision 1.3

Published By Eduardo Suastegui

A *Voice of the Mute Tales* production

http://eduardosuastegui.com

ISBN-13: 978-1516805860
ISBN-10: 1516805860

Acknowledgements

A story like this one could not even enter the imagination if not for the sacrifice of our men and women in uniform. To them and their families, I dedicate this book. And for those who came back alive, yet gravely injured, I pray for healing and restoration to the very way of life they gave so much to protect.

Chapter 1

"Ma'am, do you know how fast you were going?" the officer asks.

We're halfway there. I told Cassandra to speed, that we have dispensation. She told me, no, if we get stopped, like we are now, we'll end up wasting more time. Oh, and since she's driving, easy for me to say go ahead and speed, since she'll be the one getting the ticket. To her credit, she hasn't done the I-told-you-so routine since the patrol's flashing lights came up behind us.

"Heard of that explosion in Denver International?" I grumble at him from the front passenger seat. "We's on our way there, on the double. Orders."

From the back seat and trunk of the

4Runner, Shady and Shadow growl with their own flavor of displeasure.

The officer's hesitating now, eyeing our uniforms. I would have preferred not wearing them because they're going to make us sore thumbs in more ways than one when we arrive on scene, but we had no time to drop by home and do a quick change into our civies.

"You got some papers to confirm?" he asks.

"No, sir," Cassandra says. "We got the call, and out we went. We can produce ID, if you'd like."

I lean over and take off my black Beret. I hate what I'm about to do, but sometimes you gotta play the card you'd rather keep down.

"This here is Captain Cassandra Godinez. I'm Major Jane McMurtry. As seen on TV and the Internet."

He squints. "Oh, yeah." Now his lips break into a queasy, almost embarrassed smile. Then he turns serious. "You tracked those kids a while back, didn't you?"

Something in me stirs, threatens to give way, but I push on. "These here are U.S. Armed

Forces trained dogs, ready for duty, in this case, to clear the area of any other bombs that might be present."

Shady and Shadow back me up with more growling.

The officer nods. "OK. Follow me." He runs back to his car, and in another Colorado second we're speeding down I-25, faster than before, with emergency flashing lights parting the traffic seas for us.

I slap Cassandra on the lap. "See? All things do work for the good. Now we'll get there even faster."

"Of those who love him," she says.

"Huh?"

"In all things God works for the good of those who love Him, to them who are called according to his purpose."

I slap her on the lap again. "Well, I'm loving him just a little more right about now." With a forced chuckle I try to relax her a bit. "And we got a call this morning, so that rounds it out nicely, don't it? Even if I'm still a little fuzzy-shaky on the purpose part. But the day is still young, so hope still springs."

During the first ten miles of our drive, we listened to the news reports about the explosion at the airport—the bombing, though no one's calling it that yet. I'm figuring everything that was going to blow up has, and I'm wondering what *purpose* it serves to have us haul clear down to Denver post-haste/post-facto when all the bomb experts can do the forensics. I told Cassandra as much, right before I shut off the radio and its bleating reportage, and from the sideways glance she shoots me now, I know she's connected that with my latest bid at sarcasm.

"We're there to do a job," she says. "Maybe it seems stupid to you, but the optics of us clearing the airport, giving people the peace of mind that there aren't any more bombs going off today, that's purpose enough for me."

"Don't you think they got plenty of dogs and gear nearby, right there onsite? By the time we get there they'll have cleared that place through and through."

"What are you saying?"

"I don't know what I'm saying, if predicting the future is what you have in mind. But we ain't racing down there to clear no airport." I say that with more conviction than I ought to project. In this age of visual messaging, I wouldn't put it past the Feds to want me and Cassandra for nothing but the *optic* of having us prance around on TV with two highly trained dogs.

Cassandra's features crease into a momentary frown, and she says nothing back. That's her way of agreeing when I prove her wrong, or when she doesn't quite agree with me, but sees I'm making a semblance of a point. After a couple of months with her, I've learned at least that much about her. Usually she drops the subject, but not this time.

"So what you're saying is that there is *another* purpose."

"How do you figure?" I ask.

"Well, they wouldn't bring us in just because. I mean people and life aren't *that* irrational. If not to clear the airport, then they're calling us to do something else. Probably something no one onsite can do. Dare we say, a higher *purpose*, perhaps?"

"That sounds an awful lot like wishful thinking," I say, knowing I should do what she did a second ago: give a little ah-ha frown to acknowledge the other person has a point. For good measure I add, "And what gives with all this talk about purpose, anyway?"

"I didn't bring it up."

"And I did?"

Her lips break into one of her I gotcha grins. "Sure, with your fill-in-the-blank sentence."

It takes me a half second to catch on to her cleverness. She's pointing out that with my half-quote, half-paraphrase of that Bible verse, I suggested the rest of it in fill-in-the-blank fashion, including the purpose part.

"Do you really think that?" she asks. "That what you're doing has no purpose?"

"Oh, Lord. You're driving eighty-five to ninety, and you got the spare cycles to get mushy-philosophical on me?"

I slouch down on my seat, feeling like a sullen teenager that doesn't want to have the hard talk with her parent, but is trapped there in the car nonetheless. With my glazed, straight-ahead stare, the road blurs by, and I wonder how much this moment resembles the rest of my life, going really fast without knowing the point behind the going. Oh, I used to think I knew, but the destination and what I was supposed to do there seldom if ever turned out the way I anticipated.

As if reading me through my body language, she says, "Just because you're going somewhere fast doesn't mean the purpose won't reveal itself when you get there. You just have to be open to it."

"Open to God's leading, you mean."

She grins again, this time with one of her trying-to-be-clever grins. "I'm keeping it non-denominational and inclusive."

I shake my head at that and look away through the passenger side window. She can read me, too, and knows I'm giving her my let's-drop-it signal. She does, and we drive on in silence.

In mid-morning traffic, we have no problem

getting there in the time we promised over the phone, with a little margin to spare thanks to our police escort. However, as we approach the exit to the side road that leads into the terminals, things thicken up.

"Stay right on his six," I tell Cassandra as the cop blares his horn with screaming siren to weave his way along shoulders, sidewalks, and wherever he can find an inch to squeeze past the snarled traffic.

"I'm guessing he's been on the radio and been told he's cleared hot to get us there by whatever means necessary," Cassandra says as she struggles to keep up.

After a few maneuvers that remind me far too much of careening down a cruddy road inside a rattling Humvee, we go past the point where they're rerouting traffic out of the airport. Things clear for us, and we speed undeterred up to the first checkpoint, manned by two guys, in BDUs, body armor, and lugging semi-automatic rifles.

"Guard," Cassandra says, as in National Guard.

We stop. I see the patrol officer gesturing back toward us. It only takes a second for one of the sentries to start making a wide circular come-on-through motion. When we approach, he keeps waving us through. The other guard gives us a subtle chest salute.

"They're waiting for us," Cassandra says.

"Yeah, maybe."

"No maybe about it. Purpose is just around the corner."

We arrive at the first terminal, and the patrol car stops. Some other cop is waving at him, screaming. Cassandra pulls up right up to the patrol car's bumper, and we jump out.

"Hey, you can't be here!" the cop on the sidewalk is yelling at us.

"They're here on orders, Army specialists."

"Well, no one cleared that up with me, and this is a stay out zone. Cleared personnel only."

"That's what I'm telling you. They're cleared to be here."

"Well you sure are not."

While that keeps going on, Cassandra and I go about our business. We strap on our packs, get the dogs out, put them on leash. I hold both of them while she calls the number we got along with our orders.

"Major McMurtry and Captain Godinez reporting for duty." She listens. "Roger that." She hangs up and turns to whisper, "This way, past Mr. Didn't-get-the-memo, unfortunately."

We turn. She walks Shady. I walk Shadow.

The cop goes to get in our way. I say, "*Gib Laut*," and both dogs speak in unison, which really comes out more like some scary barking.

Our thorn in the flesh stands down.

"Thank you for your support, officer," I say as we walk past him.

Cassandra and I both travel frequently through Denver International, and with the brief directions she got on the phone, she guides us to our destination without any problem. Along the way we see several law enforcement and Federal personnel. It appears they've all received the memo, because they let us through without word.

It feels strange to walk through an empty terminal where only hints of travel remain. The stray boarding pass on the floor, strewn briefcases and carry-ons left behind, and phone chargers still hanging from wall sockets tell the story of a chaotic evacuation. Then there's the smell. It still fills the space and it stops me. Shadow whines and growls. Cassandra stops next to me, and I sense that smell hits her too, full-on like a wave of memories and anguish, the aftermath that never stays all the way behind you.

"What sicko said they love that smell in the morning or any other time of the day?" I mutter.

I look over at Cassandra again. Her jaw muscles are twitching. "Press on?" she says through gritted teeth.

"Onward and downward," I mutter back.

We enter a bridge between jet ways, and there it meets us, the random arrangement of bodies and their parts, the splattering of blood, the shattered glass, the charred, blackened point where death exploded forth.

A man in a black suit greets us. He shows us his ID from some agency I don't pay any attention to. Beyond him I see a man I do recognize, squatting down. He's using a high pitch voice to say something to a white dog, a terrier of some kind, who's tethered to a pole, next to a trashcan whose side has sheared off.

The dog barks at him, then goes into a low level growl.

"Dan," I call out.

He stands, turns to me, flashes me a half smile, then gestures for me to approach.

"Dog, or no dog?" I ask.

"Your call," he says back. "Just try not to step on anything."

I look down at the bodies and debris field to consider the incomprehensibility of that request. There's no way I can walk across and not step on something. But I get the spirit of what he's asking: disturb the scene as little as possible.

The guy next to me hands me blue booties. Six of them, so he's with it. While I slide mine over my boots, Cassandra helps me do the same with Shadow, using rubber bands she takes out of her backpack to tie off the slack.

"Is that him?" the suit next to us asks pointing at Shadow.

Figuring him and Cassandra can do the small talk thing, I ignore him and start walking. We pass the charred blast epicenter point, Shadow growling at it while I think, good, he's not freezing on me with his own kind of canine PTSD.

I've seen this before. Not much to guess at here. We got us a suicide bomber.

I keep walking. With every step I tell myself I'm in Denver. In Denver, dang it, not over there with crazies blowing themselves up. But wherever I am, something inside me threatens to give way, again, for the thousandth time. I may be in Denver, but I'm still in this world, the one where people unleash unfathomable cruelty for reasons only they can convince themselves they understand.

I press on, past three more bodies and sundry body parts. On the walls below windows that no longer have glass, I see the embedded shrapnel. Nasty stuff from the looks of it, like thin, jagged slices of metal.

"Jesus!" I say as I get to Dan.

"Joseph and Mary," he says, harking back to another time when I threw out the Savior's name, and he enumerated his earthly parents. He looks up at me from his crouched position. "You OK with this?"

"What am I here for?" I say, foregoing asking him whether he requested me or recommended I be pulled into this, because I know he did, and all I need to know now is why in God's name he'd do such a thing.

"We need your help with this little guy."

I look at the dog. Shadow's already got lock on him with his single foggy eye. It's a Jack Russel Terrier, almost solid white, with brown patches around each eye and ear. A red spot covers his chest, and I'm about to think that as an unusual trait in this breed when I realize it's blood.

He's eyeing Shadow and sniffing at the air. I'm sniffing for a reason I need to interact with him.

"Let me guess. He's an eye witness, and I'm supposed to go doggie whisperer on him to get his statement."

"No, yes." Dan rises from his crouching position. "It's more complicated than that."

"I bet it is."

"He's one of the airport's bomb sniffing dogs."

"OK."

Dan points back toward the blast epicenter. "He belonged to that guy. The handler is the guy that blew himself up."

"Alrighty, then." I stare down at what remains of whoever initiated this carnage, figuring that's how the bomb got past security. Security brought it in. Brilliant. What does this have to do with me?

I'm sure the question must show plain and clear on my face as I turn to Dan, because he rushes to get to the point.

"This dog lived with him. We think he can provide some clues in the investigation."

"How many times do I have to tell you, Dan? Dogs don't talk. I can't interview him and ask him what he saw, where his handler might have stashed any more C4 or barrels of

Nitrogen. It don't work like that."

"I know. But we'd like to take him back to this guy's apartment, see what he can help us turn up. Bomb squad's there right now."

I point at the terrier. "So take him."

"Brilliant minds think alike."

"Still not seeing where I come in."

"In case you haven't noticed, he isn't exactly being cooperative. We can grab him, stuff him in a crate, but I told people that won't do any good."

I turn back to the little guy, and he's looking up at me.

"He's not growling at you," Dan points out.

"Yeah, we're in sizzling heat for each other already," I say, regretting my words to an extent. Looking into the terrier's brown eyes, even a few feet away, I detect something there, like he's looking into my soul and imploring me to understand what he's going through. Like he knows I'll understand what he's seen, what he's feeling, because I've seen and felt it too.

"Alright, why don't you step back," I say to Dan.

I consider my choices for a moment and decide I'll go in with Shadow. I'm guessing part of whatever connection he's seeing in me has to do with his noticing there's a big, ugly lady with her dog. She might be good people.

Shadow and I take a couple of steps toward him, stopping when I hear him whine.

"It's OK," I say, turning up the pitch in my voice.

Shadow whines back as if to echo my reassurance.

We step in, nice and slow, until we're on him. I bend down and let Shadow and the terrier do the sniff introductions. Shadow towers over him, but the little guy stands his ground, looking up at him, even if his expression comes across as one of contrition. When he's satisfied with him, Shadow lays one long, wet tongue stroke on the terrier's face. I've seen him do that before with other dogs, no matter what the size. It's Shadow's "you're in" seal of approval.

Now I crouch down, thankful I elected to wear my fancy legs today, the ones that let me do this. And it's a good thing, because with this little guy, my 6′ 1″ frame needs to shrink as low as it can go.

"His name's Rover," Dan says behind me.

"Rover," I say, and the terrier perks up. "I bet you got a lot of teasing in school growing up with a name like *Rover*. But I like it. It has character. I think it may even turn into good branding for you if we get you an agent."

I reach under his chin and feel around the bloody spot on his chest. I find no cuts there, which can only mean the blood came flying from someone else. The thought shakes me, but I do what you're supposed to do when evidence of cruelty threatens to pull you back into the oppressive gloom of your memories. You face it, you settle it, you move on.

I remove my backpack and search in one of its pockets for one of the paper towels I carry. Using my water bottle, I moisten the towel almost to the soaking point and use it to rub off as much of the blood as I can get off. It turns from red, to pink, and finally to a ghostly pink you'd have to look for to notice.

Rover seems to like that, me taking care of him. Into a small cup I get out of the backpack I pour some of the water. He likes that too, lapping up all of it in seconds.

"There," I say when he looks up at me. "Feeling canine again, ain't ya?"

I cup my hand under his chin and stare into his brown eyes. Oh, boy, I see a lot of sadness in there. Yeah, and he sees mine too, don't he? He's lost his handler, I've lost my legs and much more along the way. Yeah, we get each other, don't we? Sure we do.

He whimpers, and I cry in silence. "It's all good, Rover," I whisper through a strangled throat. "Tears and crying, that's how springs of hope bust through."

I stay like that, by now on my knees, Shadow covering my right flank, the one that spans the carnage, Rover in front of me, staring back at me with sadness and purpose in his eyes. Purpose. There it is, in that little dog.

I know I'm shaking, and I know whoever's looking on can see it. And I don't care. This is who I am. Broken. Mangled. Trudging on.

"Looks like you two got a thing going," I hear Dan saying behind me, closer now, his voice trying to inject levity where there ain't none.

I undo Rover's leash and take it in my hand. "We gotta take care of business, OK?"

He looks up at me. His eyes say he'll do whatever I tell him, go wherever I take him.

I lift him under his belly and tuck him at my left, away from the blast zone. He don't need to look at that. With my right I lead Shadow by the leash and I make my way past the bodies and debris. Dan trails behind me. Ahead I can see a few more suits and uniforms have gathered. I don't take no mind to any of them. I got my hands full, thank you.

To Dan I say, "You know where we're going?"

"Yeah."

When I reach her, I tell Cassandra. "We're going to the perp's home."

"Roger that."

She follows us with Shady, and we head out, away from death and the acrid smell of death's instrument. We go out of the terminal, away from destruction and into the light and crisp, clean air of a fall Colorado morning.

"Smell that, Rover?" I tell him with a gentle squeeze. "Suck it in boy. That right there is life."

Chapter 2

On the way to the bomber's apartment, Cassandra drives while I use my cellphone in speaker mode to talk with Dan. He opts to lead with chit-chat. I learn he's turned in all his thesis papers, and he's now prepping for his dissertation. Ahead of schedule, he says, because he wanted to beat the holidays. I ask him if he has any Thanksgiving plans and tell him I've been thinking about cooking a turkey at my house. Cassandra chimes in, says she'll be there, not wanting to trek out to California until Christmas. Dan stays non-committal, but he'll do all he can to make it, he says.

That's enough preamble, so I ask Dan how he, a Boulder cop, got involved in a Denver case. It's complicated, he says, will tell me more later, "but net-net, I'm in an anti-terrorist task force." He says something about it having to do with his thesis and credits he gets toward it with field work, and I'm thinking, yeah, we need to talk about this more later, make sure I understand this thesis of his.

We arrive at our destination a little after noon. I'm hungry, so is Cassandra, so we split a granola bar to chase away the stomach growlies. When we reach the perimeter, we learn personnel is already inside, in the apartment building, looking for signs of bombs, materials and booby-trapping.

I hate this part of the job, again, because I'm just the tracker, the finder, and the idea of people tinkering with hot wires and explosives doesn't appeal to me. A busted dog at my side and two sheared off legs, you should hardly blame me for my well-earned apprehension.

The head of the bomb squad greets us. After some introductory banter, he clears me, just me, to go in with one dog. Figuring the bomb squad is already in the apartment, I tell him I want to do an outside sweep, just outside, maybe the parking structure. He says go for it, they haven't gotten to the parking structure yet.

Rover and Shady stay back with Cassandra. I take Shadow, and along with a guy from the bomb squad, we approach the front of the building. A stairway leads up to the lobby on one side, with the parking lot entrance sloping down on the other.

"Underground parking," the bomb squad guy says. "Three levels."

"And you haven't searched it yet," I reply.

"Got our hands full upstairs."

"OK, then."

I pull on Shadow's leash, and that's when I notice it. He's down on his front paws, butt sticking up in the air, face flat to the ground, pointing right at the parking entrance. He whimpers. He growls.

"*Revier*," I command him. "*Sook!*"

He ain't moving. I've seen this before, the first time I tried to exercise him with a gun powder scent. He's frozen, like that building is the upside down flower pot where I hid his prize. The prize that reminds him of getting too close to an IED and getting his eyes and hind leg shred.

"*Hierr*," I say with a pull on his leash, and we walk back to the perimeter.

From the look on Cassandra's face, she gets it. "Trade for Shady?" she asks.

That was my plan, but I catch Rover's eye. I see something sharper than sadness there. "Him."

"Him?" Cassanda asks, harking back to the discussion we had walking back to my 4Runner that we wouldn't use Rover unless his involvement became necessary.

"Yeah," I say, knowing full well you don't bring an unknown dog into a job any more than you run a race in a brand new, never-used pair of running shoes, much less strap on someone else's. But I'm thinking, guessing, really, that if there's stuff that goes boom in that underground parking garage, Rover saw it going in. Just like he saw the explosion at the terminal, when his mind-twisted handler tied him far enough from the blast so Rover could watch the slaughter of twenty-one people.

I hand off Shadow to Cassandra and take Rover's leash. Walking back to the building, I feel silly. How this must look, a brawny, tall woman leading a skinny little dog whose snappy gait becomes a white blur in order to keep up with her ungainly long stride.

For his part Rover's feeling no shame. When I look down at him he's on the job, man. He's trotting along without a shred of care of what anybody thinks, his focus on only one thing: the entrance into that parking lot. Part of me wonders how he knows I want to go there, and I can only suppose he saw me and Shadow standing there. Part of me wants to imagine he saw Shadow freeze and wants to show his big bad and black buddy how it's done.

Or, like I've already considered, he saw it. He smelled it. When his deceased master stashed it there, maybe this morning, maybe a week or a month ago. And he wants to take me to it. Because I looked into his eyes and saw his sadness, and he saw mine, and he wants to show what to do with things others have turned upside down. Sniff them out. Find them.

Root them out.

We rise up the driveway and scamper down the ramp into the parking structure. The air rises cool and damp from the concrete floor which apparently some cleaning crew hosed off earlier today. For a moment I wonder if the water will throw off the scent, but Rover presses on undeterred. He quick-steps around a puddle as he traces his route a few steps ahead of me. Down, down we go, until the first turn. Behind me I hear the steps of at least two men, bomb squad members, as we round the bend, and down, down we go again.

The next bend comes, but Rover does not take it. He pulls the leash tight, and I pick up my step seeing how he and the leash draw a line straight for a utility panel. It rises beige-gray from floor to ceiling. Rover stops by it and paws at the metal door. He sniffs and snorts at the metal corner before he sits at attention, his nose aimed right at the panel.

"Over to you," I say to the bomb squad guy closest to me. "Nunez," I say reading out his name tag. "I think we got us something big here."

He nudges me aside, and I pull Rover away. Together we back-step up the parking lot's incline. I look over my shoulder, picturing the way the scent from here must travel around the bend and back out to the street. Shadow smelled it all the way out there. That's something, I think. I didn't realize he could pick up a scent that far out. Either I'm right and that's an arsenal's worth of explosives, or Shadow came back with more than a trickster hip joint and a foggy eye that sees more than advertised.

Nunez is feeling his way along, ear against the door.

One of his buddies asks, "Hear anything?"

"Buzzing. But I'm guessing there are a lot of relays in there, anyway." With his ear still against the panel, he reaches out his hand. "Stet."

His partner hands him a stethoscope, and Nunez uses it to listen. A little bit of that, and he lets out a curse. "A literal ticker in there, dude." He points at me. "Good job, time to head up and out."

"Yes, sir," I say, and I pull on Rover's leash.

He doesn't budge.

"Come on, boy," I say, my fears now materialized. I've no idea what command set he goes by, and I sure don't want to start working my way through the ones I know, not with a ticker six feet away. I go pick him up, but he snarls at me.

"Hey!" I say. "Bad boy."

He looks up at me with an imploring look. Trust me on this, I see him telling me.

"OK, show me," I say relaxing my voice.

He pulls the leash to my left, and I follow him.

"Hey!" Nunez shouts after me. "I said out."

"He's telling me there's more," I say, not really having any confidence in that assertion, except I have this little guy pulling on me with the determination of someone who knows the scale of our trouble and desperately wants to let us know.

I'm running now, and so is Nunez behind me.

"We're going to need help, several crews working in here," I tell him. "Start radioing that in."

He shouts that to his partner at the moment Rover lets up a bit. When I turn to see, he's standing by a white van.

I go say something, but only a grunt comes out.

He goes up to it, rises on his hind legs and paws at the bumper three times, then drops down into a seated position. We're at the bottom of the garage now, and I hate to think there's more, but I have to think that way now.

I lean down. "Any more?"

He looks up at me. I have no idea what those eyes are saying, except I see nothing in there but sadness. I pick him up, tuck him under my arm. He lets me this time, and I take that for another sign he knows of no more bomb sites.

"I'm sorry, man," I say as I turn to Nunez. "You guys are going to have to diffuse two bombs in tandem, or let this building go up."

He reaches out with his arm and points me

to the staircase. "We got this." He walks me to the door, opens it up for me, gentleman-like and adds, "You done good. No shame at all in stepping off. You did your job. Now we do ours."

"Yeah, sure," I say feeling awkward.

"And thank you for your service to our country. Now, get."

I freeze for a moment, and I'm back somewhere else, in Iraq, where Shadow and I have just found a bomb, and some other guy is telling me to get the hell out of there. It ain't right. It doesn't feel like it, anyway, me leaving now, them having to face the bomb head on while I scurry away.

Nunez pushes me into the staircase, and that snaps me out enough to climb the steps, even if I'm shaking and sweating as I go. I'm hearing shouting now, lots of it, up top and down below. When I reach the street, a cop takes me by the arm, and we trot-run toward the place where I left Dan Murphy and Cassandra. Except I don't see them there, and there seem to be a lot less police and first responders around now.

The head of the bomb squad is still there.

"It's big," I tell him. "Could bring down that whole building, and then some.

"We know."

"I hope you were evacuating before we got here."

"We were. Almost there. Listen, do me a favor."

"OK."

"I told your partner to get it started, but I think you can do better. Can you draw the press to you, get them the hell away from here?"

"Will do," I tell him.

Now I'm running again, toward the press core, a cluster of shouting, cameras and other equipment. In the middle of it I see Cassandra. She looks stuck, and by my estimation, we're not far enough.

"Folks!" I shout. "Follow me. I have some news for you."

They say that if you think you're a leader, you turn around and no one's following, well, you thought wrong. After a few strides past the crowd of reporters, I steal a look back. They're giving chase, and I guess at least for now I have my answer.

When we've gone another block and a half, I stop and turn to face them. They enclose the space around me like a black hole sucks up matter. I look around for Cassandra, desperate for her to join us. For her safety, yes, but also because over the last couple of months, when we went out on three searches that turned out to be pretty straight-forward, she and I have done tandem news conferences where I start off with a couple of facts, then let her handle the tricky, land-mine questions. We've done pretty good at that. She likes to joke she's Aaron to my Moses.

Questions are flying at me, and I'm feeling a little overwhelmed—OK, a lot, as in buried. Finally one question I can latch to rises above the cackling of the others.

"Ms. McMurtry, can you tell us why you chose to take that little dog you're holding instead of your own. Is it true that he belongs to the man that set off the bomb in Denver International?"

I raise my hand like the student that says, yes, teacher, I can actually answer that one.

"Alright, let me say up front that this is still an ongoing investigation, and anything I share with you good folks is preliminary and subject to change upon further findings." That there comes out pretty good, I say to myself, a line Cassandra made me memorize. As she's still not at my side—though I see she's getting close—I opine I handled that rather well, thank you.

"Yeah, but why did you take him?"

"All's I'll say for now is that this little fellow right here is more capable than his debonair looks may suggest." I let them laugh at that a little, a much needed bit of levity in a moment following carnage and laced with impending doom. "As it turns out, he's familiar with the explosives used at the airport, since he was on the scene there, so we thought he could help us at this location."

There's some fibbing in there, but of the

good kind. I really don't want to get into the bomber's identity or Rover's connection to him. I'm pretty sure I'll be bobbing in boiling water if I go there. It's not my place, anyway, and one thing I've learned in my short stint as a law enforcement assistant is to know my place and heap mounds of deference on the folks in charge. That keeps the jobs coming and the checks clearing.

A bunch of other questions are flying at me now, none of which I can really make out, and that's when Cassandra reaches me, pulling on two leashes, one arm up in the air.

"Please, guys, one question at a time," she says.

"Can you tell us whether you found explosives in there?"

"That is still under investigation. The folks from the bomb squad are working it right now."

"You went in and came out pretty quick. Does that mean you did find something?"

"No, it could mean anything," I say, knowing that's anything but the right answer.

"Well, what does it mean?"

"It means," Cassandra says jumping in, "what Major McMurtry said in her previous answer. The bomb squad is investigating to make a final determination."

"What about your bigger dog? You went in with him first, but you stopped at the entrance. Is that normal, and what does it mean?"

"It was an inconclusive finding," Cassandra replies. "This is why Major McMurtry tried a different approach."

"But why not go in with the little dog first, if that made better sense, like you said a couple of questions ago."

"We follow a protocol," Cassandra jumps in again. "That protocol calls for using our dogs first."

The reporters think they have a juicy bone we're not letting them chew on completely, so they keep gnawing on us. I start tuning them out.

My height allows me to look over them, and I'm seeing something I don't like. A lot of law enforcement uniforms running out of the building. When that goes on for more than a minute, I raise my hand.

They go quiet, and I say, "Folks, this would be a good time to take cover."

It takes them a couple of seconds to catch my meaning. Once they get it, all cameras point back to the building while those of us with more sense and less drive to get killer video of a building exploding search for solid places to take shelter.

Chapter 3

The building never goes off. I will learn an hour later they ran everyone out while a couple of rolling drones did the deed. After some digging and another hour, I also learn things came very close to a big boom, hence the panicked running. Still, by evening, the news is reporting a big success story against a tragic start for the day, and Jane McMurtry's brand is splattered all over the place, with lots of video footage of her, her Army partner, and the pack of dogs. I even see a snippet of me going into and coming out of the airport. No clue how they got that, but man, my agent is texting me that my Twitter feed and Facebook page are going nuts, nuts, nuts!

I feel numb to it all, here, propped up with a

stack of pillows on my hotel bed, while Cassandra channel surfs from the other bed. The dogs, Rover included, are snoring with conviction, each of them to their own pitch and rhythm. I'd laugh if I didn't feel so deflated.

"We did good today," Cassandra repeats for the tenth time, I think. "*You* did good."

"Yeah, maybe."

"You don't see how you made a difference today?"

"Let's not do the pep rally thing right now. Please."

She allows about a minute of silence before she starts up again with, "You're tired. How about some room service?"

"Sounds swell."

Over the next few minutes, Cassandra does a reading from the room service menu. When I make my choices, she makes the call. Once done with that she comes back to sit on her bed, the side closest to me, elbows on her knees, bending down at the back.

"You and Dan didn't say much face to face," she notes.

"It was a busy few hours."

"You two haven't talked much lately."

"It's been a few busy months, for Dan, especially, school and all."

"He seemed friendly enough on the phone."

I turn to her. "Like he's still interested, you mean?"

"Still? Has the guy given you a reason to think otherwise?"

"Are you going Allison on me, Cassandra? Seems a little under your pay grade."

"Allison's right. You should snag this guy. Seems decent enough, and for the quiet type, he's sure not being reserved about how he feels about you."

"I invited him for Thanksgiving, didn't I?"

"Thanksgiving's nearly two months away. What's wrong with getting together before then?"

"Where's the fire?" I ask.

"A more appropriate question is, where's the molasses? Why all the waiting?"

I restrain my urge to snap at her. "Look, Cassandra. I appreciate the girl-to-girl concern, but—"

"You're not ready?"

"Yeah, maybe."

"OK, I'll just say this, and I'll drop it because you're right. I'm not Allison, and I'm not going to hound you on this. But sometimes there's no being ready. Waiting doesn't help. You just have to jump and pull the ripcord. You know that. You've been there. You've done it, jumped into crazy things when your head screamed at you that you're not ready. And this isn't that crazy."

"I guess it isn't."

She nods and lowers her voice. "You can still go easy. Be cautious. But be fair, too. I'm looking at Dan, and he's not looking happy with waiting and waiting on you."

I avert my eyes in the direction of the TV. "Thanks. Got it." I cross my arms and immediately feel like a pouty kid. Stupid. Stubborn. Filled with nonsense.

"He's in town, in some hotel," she says.

"I thought you were just going to say the other thing and drop it."

"Wouldn't hurt to have our dinner, call him in the meantime, go down to the bar, right here in the hotel for drinks or something. Doesn't have to be a late night. He'll get that. That you need your rest." She pauses. "I can join in, if you'd like."

"Who's going to take care of the dogs?" I ask.

"Oh, yeah. Right. Guess I have to stay here with them, then. I'll also take them for their evening poop run."

When I turn to face her again, she's grinning.

"Nice," I say. "Real smooth."

"Call him?"

I pick up my cell and appease her.

For the first few minutes, I wonder if meeting Dan for drinks is a good idea. First of all, neither of us is much of a drinker. I'm nursing a clear white glass of wine, and he's doing likewise with a beer, neither of us lowering the top line on our glasses much. Second, and most concerning, we're both clearly wiped out, and for the first few minutes we trade inanities rising a hairline's worth of interest above how's the weather.

After a few rounds of that, I aim to break the verbal impasse with the first substantial question. "You angling for a job with the Feds?"

"That obvious?"

"Yeah, maybe. How many people have asked you that question?"

He grins the way he does when he thinks my intelligence "breaks through my deceptive folksy act," as he said a couple of months back.

"You're the first," he says.

I search for my next comment or question, a pang of apprehension sweeping through me. What if he gets a job in DC or some other place that requires more than an hour's drive?

"Anything firm yet?" I ask.

"Yeah, maybe," he replies with yet another of his grins, the one he reserves for when he manages to use my favorite two word response. "Here in Denver, actually."

"That's nice."

"That relieved?"

Now I grin. "I like to keep my enemies close."

"Ouch."

"Didn't say you's one of them. But if the shoe fits…"

"I like it here in Colorado," he says. He seems to hesitate the way someone does when about to cross the line. "I like Colorado gals, too. One in particular."

At this point, if I want to keep up the clever repartee, I can point out I'm technically a Wyoming girl. But I fear that would force him to the brink, and do I really want him to tell me I'm the girl?

So I smile, take a sip from my wine, look for an escape tangent.

"How much go-boom stuff did they find?" I ask.

"I don't want to talk about work. I've been up to my neck in this since 7 AM this morning, and after seeing what we saw today, we need a break. Don't you think?"

"Guess you're right." I say that not quite liking the harsh tone in his voice, the way he's cut me off, even if I can understand why. It ain't nice to look over a field of bodies, then relive it over wine and a beer.

"When's your dissertation?" I ask.

"December fifth."

"And then you're a free man. Free to pursue the dream."

"Sure. Let's call it that." He pauses for a moment and in his eyes I see he wants to take the conversation in a different direction. "You seem to be doing good."

"Is that what you think? The way little Rover turned me into a weepy mess?"

"I like that about you."

"That I'm a weepy mess?" I ask.

"That you're living through your heart."

I see his hand moving toward mine, and I flinch. He stops.

"Am I, living through my heart?" I ask as much to keep the conversation rolling as to diffuse the awkwardness.

"In some ways you are. Maybe in others

you're not ready yet. It's normal. It's understandable."

"Ought'a give you a PhD for that little pearl right now."

Dan looks away, over at the bar, as if he can find the next words inscribed in one of them bottles lining up the upper shelf. He keeps his gaze there, and I sense he's contemplating whether to go heavier or back off.

"Is Thanksgiving a definite go?" he asks.

"Yeah. I don't see why not. God willing and all that, but I promise to shop for a juicy turkey. I'll brine it and all. How's that sound?"

He turns back with a sad smile. "Sounds great. Count me in, and let me know what I can bring."

I clink his beer with my class ring. "Some of this, since you're not fond of much else."

"Will do." He takes a deep breath before adding, "I should go. I'm really beat. Gotta get ready for that briefing tomorrow. You'll be there, right?"

"Wouldn't miss it. Thanks for coming."

"Thanks for calling."

We get up and give each other a sideways hug, the kind that ain't supposed to touch anything vital or sensitive and ends up feeling fake and not worth the awkwardness. Then he walks off, head down, never looking back.

I retake my seat and contemplate whether to finish my glass, decide not to, but stay there in that dim booth nonetheless. I scan the bar and the surrounding tables. Plenty of men there, none I like, and more to the point, none that look at me. As in not at all, zero.

It dawns on me a few seconds ago I had a man across from me that did little but look at me. He didn't even drink from his beer, which sits across from my glass, nearly untouched. I stare at its amber color, now losing its froth, and I feel a deep sadness well up inside me.

I push my wine glass up to Dan's beer glass until they touch with a dull clink. Under the incandescent light above the table, the wine turns to the color of beer. I suppose this might make a great illustration for the fusing of two lives: fundamentally different but coming together to give the impression of sameness.

Chapter 4

I hate briefings for the same reason I hate wasting my time inside classrooms and lecture halls. Ain't got the heart or attention span for it. Yet, if like me you've done business with the military or the Feds, you've had your fair share of death by bullet point pontification. As the 9 AM briefing gets rolling in the Denver FBI headquarters, I buckle up for yet another bore fest of the sort I hoped to have left behind.

Some FBI honcho stands up first, down there in this small auditorium. Cassandra and I watch from the back row, where I insisted we sit in case she or I have to go check on the dogs, currently residing in a small conference room down the hall. Listening to the windbag in the front makes me wish I had my cellphone on me, maybe check what my favorite Hollywood movie stars are doing or whether they're out of rehab yet. But our phones stayed locked up outside the office area, a secured one that bans all types of recording or transmitting electronics.

I shift in my seat as the next guy comes up. Like a slow motion machine gun, he rattles through the details of the case: the time of the incident, the size and impact of the explosion, the preliminary findings for the types of explosives used, how they matched the explosives found in and around the bomber's apartment. He closes with the working theory that the bomber had accomplices. This determination, he explains, results from the lack of evidence that the bomber himself procured any of the equipment and chemicals found in his apartment. Someone supplied him, and now the job at hand must focus on finding those suppliers, our presenter says with more life and excitement than he's shown thus far.

"Questions?" he offers and gets no takers, from which I deduce we all want what I want:

this thing to be over.

"Very well, then. Let me introduce Deputy Dan Murphy of the Boulder Police Department. We're lucky to have him on our task force. Deputy Murphy comes to us with a Bachelor's in Psychology, a Masters in Criminology and is finishing off his PhD. He very recently turned in his thesis, which I'm sure he's really glad about."

A bit of polite laughter sounds out, mostly in the front of the room. Dan stands and moves toward the podium. My heart skips a beat, as I didn't expect Dan to be doing the presenting. But there he is, big man on campus.

"The topic of his thesis makes us very glad to have him on our team," the FBI agent is saying. "That topic? The connection between the serial criminal mind and that of the terrorists." He pauses. "But I'm sure I've mangled that. You can ask Dan all about it after the briefing."

More polite laughter follows, and Dan smiles as he takes the podium. He waves for the FBI agent to remain by his side, saying,

"Actually, I'd like to have more of a discussion from this point on, and Agent Zedinski can answer some of the questions that may come up. I'd also like to point out that I'm the spokesman for a team of folks, investigators, analysts and profilers, many of who I see sitting in this room and who have gathered much of the information we're about to see regarding our suspect."

A picture and a name appear on the screen. To his credit, Dan doesn't read the name. Instead, he pauses letting us read it for ourselves. "Walid Al-Sem."

"His name, also Waleed, means reborn," Dan says. "Mr. Al-Sem is a naturalized Iraqi national. He came to the states after serving as a translator during the early post-Sadam Hussein years. His life and that of his family were in danger for his cooperation, and the U.S. government provided him asylum and fast-tracking of his resident papers and eventually his citizenship status. Mr. Al-Sem became estranged from his wife, and she and his children remained in Iraq. He lived here alone with, so far as we can tell, no connections to any other Iraqis or foreign nationals. During the last year, he's been working in the airport's bomb detection unit alongside his dog, who we now have in our custody."

He steals a look in my direction, and I give him a faint smile, wondering if he can see it this far away. I'm smiling also because while two charts have flipped behind him with the details he's given, he's told it all looking out into the audience, without reading from the charts or any notes, one hundred percent in his own words.

My smile fades as Dan relays the current working theory regarding the bomber's motivation, namely that he was under duress of some sort, probably arising from a threat against his family back in Iraq.

Something flips inside me, and I'm back in Iraq, looking over my shoulder and all around at the Iraqi nationals inside the Green Zone, wondering which of them is going to do us next. I can feel it, the Iraqi sun beating down on me, the smell of the sandy dust all around us, the beads of sweat sifting down from my helmet's head strap, and most of all, my fear.

"They want to blow away our trust," I blurt out. Next to me, Cassandra seems to have suffered a jolt. "They're doing it again, making us feel we can't be safe anywhere."

Most of the heads in the auditorium turn around. At the front, the head honcho that got the briefing rolling half stands, fiddling with his suit jacket as if he's going to button it up.

"I'm sorry," he says. "Major McMurtry, is it? Did you have something to share?"

I stand up. "They're working from the inside, with people we think we can trust. Like this guy, doing security for a major airport, for bomb detection, even, and he's the one that blows it up. They let us train 'em, feed 'em, put uniforms on their backs. They walk among us, and then one night, just when we're feeling nice and cozy, they come in to our room, crawl into the bunk with us, whisper something about Allah in our ears, and blow us all to hell. Now they're bringing the same game here."

The room goes quiet. Behind me, where I'm

guessing no one can see, Cassandra is squeezing my hamstring. I've said enough. Time to sit back down.

"Yes, well," the head honcho says. "I'm sure our team has this covered."

I sit down, the stupid big girl in the class, again.

"That is one line of inquiry we'll take under advisement," Dan says, the kind thing to say. E for effort. F comes next in the alphabet.

He allows a short pause, then rejoins whatever line of reasoning he was chasing before my interruption. He goes on about this or that other thing. I'm hearing none of it. My face is getting hot, and my chest is pounding. Though Cassandra whispers in my ear that she thinks I have a point, I have none of that either. I need to get out.

I almost tackle the door on my way out. Outside, with Cassandra at my side, the dude guarding the door questions the wisdom of leaving the briefing so soon.

"Gotta check my Facebook page, see what my fans are posting on my wall this morning." I brush past him and go into the conference room where our dog pack awaits. Rover comes up running first, and I kneel down to pick him up. Shadow and Shady surround me in another second, and I realize how I belong with them, how they accept and look up to me, and how much they mean to me.

My eyes want to cry, but my chest refuses. Instead it swells with fun and joy, with their unconditional, unwavering love.

Behind me I hear the door click shut.

"You OK?" Cassandra asks.

"More than OK," I tell her at the very moment Rover reaches up and lays a wet tongue lick on me.

Dan comes into the conference room an hour later.

"Wanted to touch base with you," he says.

"Shoot."

He scans the room, looking for the dogs.

"Cassandra and I are heading home after

lunch. She took the dogs out. Went to check her sequestered cellphone."

"Oh, well. That's OK." He says that with more fluster than I usually see from him.

"What's up?" I say.

"What you said in there. I've been thinking about it. You made a good point."

"Didn't feel like anyone thought so."

"I did. Said so right then, didn't I?"

"Come on, Dan. I know a pat on the head when I get one."

"That's not—"

"No worries, big guy. I know how the game is played. Gotta impress them higher uppers. Big career opportunities ahead. Never mind the big dumb-looking chick with the hick accent."

"You know that's not what I'm all about."

"Hell, do I?"

He narrows his eyes. "You should know me well enough to know that's not who I am."

I give him a muted grin, probably more like a faint grimace. "Maybe not yet. But it's who you'll become if you hope to get ahead among all them suits."

We stare each other down, and I'm guessing he's not enjoying the way I'm looking at him anymore that I'm taking a liking to the way he looks at me.

The door opens, and Cassandra comes in with my canine triad. She looks like she has something to say, but before she gets it out, I ask Dan about Rover, whether the task force really means for me take him home.

"Until we need him again. No one really here to take care of him," Dan says. "Like we explained earlier."

I nod at that before I turn to Cassandra. "Anything to share?"

"Your agent left me a text and a voicemail message," she says. "She's been trying to reach you all morning, and since she couldn't get you... Anyway, she'd like you to do an interview with Bridget Suarez, you know, the investigative reporter. Says she's available for lunch if you are."

Cassandra and Dan trade a look I don't quite like.

"What?" I ask.

"You've heard of her, right? Bridget Suarez?" Dan asks.

"Can't say as I have," I reply. "Oh wait, she was there at that trailer park," I add, remembering the last job Dan and I worked together.

"She's the one," Cassandra says.

"Seemed harmless enough," I reply.

"In my book she's the stay away kind," Dan tells me.

"He's right," Cassandra puts in. "She likes to expose military projects, did something on Cyber surveillance recently. Scuttlebutt is that she leaked some sensitive, classified info."

"You must have heard about that," Dan says.

I wave my hands. "I've told you guys. I ain't the evening news or newspaper kind."

Dan shakes his head. "Well, my guess is that she wants to pump you about the bombing."

"Fine," I say. "We call her, tell her absolutely no discussion about an ongoing investigation, see how much of a hankering she has for lunch after that."

As we walk out we return to the Rover topic. Cassandra tells me we got paperwork authorizing us to take him with us. That's good, I reply, because I like the little guy. But I've been hesitating on whether to take him. He doesn't exactly fit the kind of dog I train or go for, even if he seems sharp and eager enough. Still, he's looked into my eyes and I've looked into his to forge a connection I can't easily dismiss. Besides, if I end up with him permanently, maybe Allison will take him. She's been looking for a small dog.

I'm hatching all those eggs in my mind, when Cassandra switches subjects on me.

"You really think it's a good idea to do the interview?"

"With your compatriot Ms. *Suah-Rezz*? Sure. Why not? Gotta keep my brand alive and my agent happy."

We've reached the car, and we take a few moments to settle the dogs in.

"What if she wants to ask about the other thing?" Cassandra asks as we climb into the front.

"What other thing?"

"What we do."

"What we do? Everybody knows what we do. That's the point, ain't it? Too keep them excited about all the awesomeness we bring to bear with our dogs."

"Not that."

"Well, what then?"

Cassandra points down at my legs.

"How would she know about that?" I ask.

"The same way she knew about the Cyber stuff."

"You mean that stuff you and Dan were talking about in there?"

Cassandra shakes her head. "You really should keep up with current events. Especially if you're going to go a few rounds with the likes of Suarez."

"I'm sure it'll be fine," I say, all the while getting the vibe I shouldn't be so sure about that.

Cassandra shrugs, and I make the call to my agent. Absolutely no discussion about the bombing, I tell her, and she says Ms. Suarez has already agreed to those ground rules. The phone was on speaker, and when I look at Cassandra, she's giving me that I-told-you-so look of hers.

Chapter 5

By the time we get to the agreed location, a Tex-Mex place in downtown Denver, Bridget Suarez is already waiting for us. Noticing her thin, tall build, long blond hair and green eyes, I can't help but ask the politically incorrect question of how her birth certificate came to list the wrong surname. Well, I don't voice it quite that way, but I get my point across nonetheless.

"Hispanics are a diverse and non-homogeneous lot," she replies with a wide smile as shiny-fake as a titanium dollar. "And please, call me Bridget," she adds with drippy pleasantness.

We ask for an outdoor table on account of our canine crew, and we find one where I can sit across from Bridget, with Shady and Shadow down below, but sitting tall to my left and Bridget's right, while Rover tucks himself around my feet. Cassandra sits last, having made a call back to our base public affairs office to let them know about the interview. With a slight nod of the head, she lets me know she took care of it. I guess we should have done that before I agreed to the interview, but I don't like my life managed that way.

"So, you two lead an interesting life," Bridget says. To Cassandra she adds, "Now, you're still in all the way, as they say, not a reservist like Jane."

"That's correct," Cassandra replies, only a tad less laconic than if she'd said, "yes." She's told me that there is no better way to annoy a reporter than to answer with straight yes and no when they keep asking yes/no questions. Cassandra says that's one of her pet peeves with interviewers these days: they ask you a yes/no question and expect you to answer as if they'd asked an open-ended question.

"And you're Air Force, not Army?" Bridget asks her.

"That's right."

I sit back, restraining the urge to ask whether this is my interview, and if so, why all the questions directed at Cassandra.

"Now, from what I read in Social Media, it was your idea for the two of you to train for the Marine Marathon in DC?"

"The Marine *Corps* Marathon," Cassandra replies. "Yes, I suggested it."

"What made you decide to do it?" Bridget asks, still directing her questions to Cassandra.

"Because it's there," I can't resist to reply.

Cassandra smiles at me. "Yeah, I've been wanting to do it for some time, and when the topic came up, I suggested it to Jane. She's been doing some very physically challenging things lately, and we agreed her training for this would help with her recovery."

Bridget looks at me. "Yes, that's quite a story, isn't it? How you can hike and manage all the physicality your job requires." She raises her index finger. "But, before we go there, you're running with your dogs?"

"Yes," I say.

To my chagrin, Cassandra elucidates with, "Only for the last ten miles, though. They'll join us at mile sixteen. Running on asphalt for longer will hurt their pads." She taps the palm of her upraised right hand.

Bridget turns to the dogs, and I love the way they're sitting right now. Their ears point straight up, as if to record every nuance of our conversation. Their snouts point right at her.

Bridget shifts a tad in the opposite direction and looking back at us says, "Shadow and Shady. Tell me about their names."

Cassandra turns to me letting me know this one's all mine.

"They were both in the Shadow class, twenty dogs in all. We thought naming it Shadow was cute, like, my dog is my shadow? Anyway, he was Shadow-7, she was Shadow-19. Only eight dogs from that class made the cut: 1, 3, 7, 10, 11, 13, 15, and 17, if I recall correctly."

"I'm sure you do," Bridget replies in a way that tells me she already has that information.

I go on. "When I got back, she was doing

therapy dog duty at the VA, and making a mess of it on account of her hyper temperament. They released her in my care, us going back and all, thinking maybe she could help me get back on my feet." I pause for a second unable to restrain the memories of how Shady has helped me and the emotion that evokes.

"I renamed her," I add. "I thought Shady sounded nicer for a girl."

"Wow, that's an awesome story," Bridget says. She swallows in a way that for once speaks of her sincerity. "And she did end up being a pretty good therapy dog for you, didn't she? Got you through some dark times."

Now something catches in my throat. "Yeah, I suppose she did."

I look over at Shady, who turns to me, tongue hanging out. I stare her down, and she turns her snout back in Bridget's direction.

Bridget frowns a bit and asks, "Why are they looking at me so intently?"

"Because they think you're really interesting, I suppose," I reply. "Or because I told them to."

A pause follows, one that neither Cassandra nor I break. Let it be tense, I figure. Let her know this isn't a push-over fishing expedition, if that's what she's after.

The waiter arrives with glasses of water and offers to take our orders. I've been hankering for some guacamole, so I order us an appetizer of that and chips. The thin crispy kind, I tell him.

He asks if he can take the rest of our order, and we realize we haven't even cracked open the menus. Making the poor guy stand there, at Bridget's insistence, we glance through the menu, ask him a barrage of questions—mostly coming from Bridget, on account of her refined, health conscious palate—and finally place our order. By the time he walks away, I'm making a note to forward his name to the Vatican along with a sainthood nomination form.

"Now, about Shadow," Bridget says. "He had to stay behind when you came home."

"Yup, still on duty," I reply. "Like any other soldier, has to serve out his tour and complete his service until discharged." Unless a bullet or a bomb changes the equation, I almost add, but decide not to.

"He came home early due to his own injuries. Serious ones, right?"

"Serious enough he got early retirement," I say.

"But looking at him, he seems to be doing well. Quite well, in fact."

"Yeah, if a shut slit for one eye and a cloudy one for the other sounds like *quite well* to you."

"He seems to see well enough," Bridget says.

"He sees you alright," I reply.

"He's really a beautiful animal," she says, going to pet him. Her hand shrinks back to her when Shadow's throat emits a low grade rumble.

"You should have seen him before. When those dark chocolate eyes of his could peer right into you. No more of that now. Just a cloud left in the one. Kind'a symbolic of how many of us come back, ain't it? All clouded up inside."

Bridget swallows and casts her sea of green gaze on me. I wonder what she sees in this long, wide face, but in hers I see something other than someone trying to play one on me.

"That's both beautiful and sad," she says.

"Hope it goes in your story, though as I don't see you writing anything down, I wonder where all our verbal calories are going."

"I have a good memory," she says with a smile. She taps on her phone. "And a recorder app. I hope your agent relayed this is how I work?"

"Dear Candice forgot that part, but that's alright." I dip a chip in the guacamole. "From the sound of your questions, it sounds like you're after a human interest story. Ain't that a tad light and fluffy for ya?"

Her smile expands. "I'd love to write any kind of story on you, human interest or otherwise. My bosses figured I needed a little variety, to branch out a bit. I specialize in military-related topics, and I guess you do have that background."

"For better or for worse."

"Going back to the marathon, I'm really impressed that Shadow can even go one mile, given the injury he sustained to his hind leg and hip."

"He's made a full recovery," Cassandra says.

"Yes," I put in. "One with lots of cloudiness in it. We're never fully recovered. More like we develop a stack of work-arounds for our dysfunctions."

"Hmm, I suppose that's even truer of you," Bridget says. "I must say when I read stories of you hiking up mountains and training for marathons, with a run at the Olympic team in the shot put, I'm amazed. Humbled, really, that I whine about going out for my morning three miler."

Cassandra and I exchange a look like two platoon buddies inching up to a mine field's perimeter.

"You know," Bridget presses. "I've heard rumors of a secret government program to develop mechanized joints and prosthetics to deal with the increasing number of vets that come back from war with serious physical injuries."

She pauses there, dangling the bait. Cassandra and I give her our best poker faces.

Bridget winks at me. "It's all very hush-hush, early development stuff. Still, it makes me wonder how much better you and Shadow would do with that sort of technology." She stops to let her twinkling green eyes dwell on me. "Or maybe you're doing better enough already."

Chapter 6

Toward the end of our lunch, my cellphone keeps buzzing, and I keep ignoring it. By the time we leave the restaurant, I have three texts and one voicemail message from Allison.

"Call me, we need to talk," each of them says, except the voicemail also conveys the urgency in Allison's voice.

I call Dan Murphy first, make sure there isn't anything he needs from us before we set out in a northerly direction. He says, no, "*vaya con Dios.*"

I hang up and call Allison. She tells me little, only that she wants to talk in person. When I press her for what's the matter, she says she has to run off, and that she'll see me at the house in an hour.

"Something wrong?" Cassandra asks.

"Allison, being her drama queen self."

"You say that like you don't mean it."

"Yeah, maybe. I don't know." I bite my lip, wishing we could blow the speed limit as much as we did on the way to Denver two days before, but I'm guessing the only police escort we'll get this time would drag us off to jail.

"Probably nothing," I add.

Perhaps sensing my angst or in spite of it, Cassandra does do a little speeding of the careful kind. We arrive at the ranch short of an hour after we left the restaurant and find Allison rocking on the front porch.

"What's up?" I ask.

"What's that?" she says pointing at our newest dog pack member.

"Rover, meet Allison. Allison, meet Rover."

"Rover," she says making a face.

"What? Isn't he cute?"

"What's he doing here?"

"Long story," I say. "Now, you had something to say?"

She twists her lips, looks at Cassandra then

back at me. "Can we go for a walk? Maybe bring your binoculars and the dogs?"

I mull that over for a moment before I ask Cassandra if she minds unpacking and taking care of Rover. What are we doing? Oh, bird watching, I whisper to her. Allison probably saw some bird she thinks is endangered, and wants to show it to me. That's why the binoculars. Cassandra winks at me and says, fine, you guys go do *that*.

Like we did a while back, Allison and I walk through the back trail behind the house and out to the small hill and its aspen trees. Once there I scan our surroundings and place Shadow and Shady on guard duty. Allison and I stand inside the trees, and this time she's the one with a secret to tell.

"Some guys came asking questions," Allison says straight away. "Came to the lab while I was working there."

"FBI?"

"DIA. Defense Intelligence something."

"They showed you ID?"

"I'm not stupid, Jane."

"What did they want to know?"

"They said they were there running your annual security check. Didn't ask much, though. Whether I think you're in financial trouble. Do you break the law, and so on. Fifteen minutes tops."

"OK, sounds innocent enough. That's normal. I told you that might happen from time to time."

"Here's the thing, though. This morning I go in to check my work email from my house, and I can't get in. Server down. I call the IT guy, and he says they've had a major server crash. And not just the main server, but the backups. Two of them. All down."

"OK," I say, though by now I'm inching up to the reason why, no, we're not OK.

"I call two hours later, because, you know, still no email, and the IT guy says that whatever hit them has wiped out everything. Every file. Completely unrecoverable. Now, remember." She lowers her voice. "This is the guy that recomposed our MRI files out of binary scraps, right? But now, nothing. Poof. All gone. Not only that, but the backup tapes he keeps? Wiped clean, too, like someone ran a huge magnet on them. His words, not mine."

I stay silent.

"You get it, right? Those guys? They weren't there to question me. They were there to get inside and do whatever they needed to do to come back that night and wipe those files. More to the point, *our* files. Get it?"

Yeah, I'm getting it, but I still don't want to. "Let's think this one nice and cool."

"What? Am I sounding a little paranoid?" She opens her eyes wide, like she's daring me to say, yes, she's coming across a little nutty like.

"There's a lot of jumping to conclusions there, Allison. Whatever happened in your lab could have any number of explanations none of which tie back to some MRI files we took. How do you know they're related?"

She takes one step back and puts hands to hips. "Maybe because I came by your house this morning to deliver your dog food shipment, and what do I see when I get here? Same two guys that questioned me, rummaging through your house." Her eyes go wide again.

I rub my forehead and close my eyes. When I reopen them, she's still looking at me, eyes near to bulging.

"That good enough of a connection for you? Ready to believe they're looking for the files? Which by the way, where did you put the disc I gave you? In a fortress, I hope."

I react more than think. A second later Allison, the dogs, and I are running back to the house. When I get there, I enter the garage, already open since Cassandra unloaded some of our gear there.

I stop and look around. Nothing seems amiss at first. Everything seems to remain as I left it. I go in the house, and with Cassandra at my heels asking what's wrong, I come to the same determination. They searched the place without leaving a trace.

I point at Cassandra. "You and I will talk in a second."

Back in the garage, I walk toward my gun safe. I examine its two keyed locks. Nothing out of the ordinary, I decide, until I take a closer look with a magnifying glass. I find scratches, the kind that a lock pick might leave. With my own keys I open the safe. My guns, my ammo, even the target sheets I keep in there, all stand and stack where I left them.

I turn my attention to a knee high stack of magazines next to the safe, atop which I affixed a sheet of paper that reads "RECYCLE." Allison lends me her pocket knife, and I use it to cut the twine that binds the bundle, thinking to myself that if someone had done the same, I would know it.

When I hand the knife back to Allison, she's smiling. "Clever," she says. "In plain sight."

"Something like that," I say, eyeing Cassandra, who is standing in the doorway that goes from the garage to the kitchen.

Returning my attention to the stack of magazines, I count five from the bottom and take out that one I'm after.

Allison's smile grows with recognition. "It's in there?"

Without opening the magazine, I can feel the disc she concealed in there. I hand her the magazine before I turn my attention to the gun safe.

From it I take out a semi-automatic rifle and snap a clip into it.

I turn to Cassandra. "Got your car keys on you?"

"For yours, not mine."

"Get yours."

"Why?"

"Because you have two minutes to leave before I turn you into Swiss cheese." I point the rifle at her.

"What the—? What's going on here?" Cassandra asks.

"What's going on here is that you knew they were coming to sniff out my house. You did, didn't you?"

"I have no idea what you're talking about."

"Fifteen seconds gone, just like that. Tick, tock."

Cassandra looks at me, and something in her eyes tells me she's decided further objections will do her no good.

I follow her in the house, rifle butt against

my shoulder, eye tracing down the sighted barrel, and I watch her retrieve the keys to her car from the kitchen counter. She turns to me one last time.

"I had nothing to do with this. I'm not here to snoop or report on you. That's not my mission."

"Oh, and what exactly was your mission, Captain Godinez?"

"As stated. To look after your needs."

I want to believe that, but I can't afford to. "Get out."

"Yes, ma'am," she says in a rather sing-songy tone.

"When you reach the other side," I tell her, "make sure to tell Brady I got it. Just like he thought. Tell him to come get it, warrant or no warrant. Second amendment before fourth, it will come to ugly blows if he tries it."

"Yes, ma'am," she says again, and just for that I want to shoot her right there and then.

I follow her out to the porch and stand there as she drives away.

"And now what?" Allison asks behind me.

"Now you leave too."

"I don't feel right doing that."

"Maybe not. But it's the only thing for you to do."

"What about you? What are you going to do?" she asks.

"That would be telling."

Thirty minutes later, I walk back after leaving my tractor and a trailer loaded with firewood blockading the main gate and the only road into my ranch. In my pocket I carry a couple of spark plugs from the tractor. They'll have to bulldoze their way in if they decide to come that way.

Shady and Shadow, now strapped with body armor, sit on either side of me on the porch. Rover has no body armor, and for that reason will stay inside the house until the festivities reach their bitter end. Wearing body armor of my own, I sway back and forth on my rocker, semi-auto rifle on my lap, and two shotguns at my feet.

How appropriate, I think, that I'm still wearing my BDUs, even if they are beginning to stench up after two solid days of wear.

Night will soon fall upon us, and to meet its darkness, a set of night vision goggles sit atop the table next to me. Without putting them on, I can still look through them onto a place far from here and yet only a memory away.

As darkness surrounds me, I sway myself to stay awake. The stench from my uniform, a mix of frozen sweat and caked on, crusted blood serves the same purpose. Five hours ago, the platoon a fellow dog handler and I were assisting sustained heavy casualties. No one's dead, but after one other ranger and I did our best to patch them all up, he and I stand alone between them and those who wait for nightfall to come finish us off. He, sniper specialist Roger Morris, has taken position up above, from where he tells me he can control the one and only road into our shattered, bloody camp.

We also have the two dogs, Shadow-7, my Shadow, and Shadow-13, A.K.A. Lucky. They will guard our flanks. Lucky, dressed in full body armor, sits higher up along the cliff side, not far from where Roger chose to build his sniper's hide. Shadow stands guard to my right, looking up to the high pass part of the road, should any enemies somehow circumvent us to approach us from there.

But our main focus lies down trail, where two hours ago, after the first bloody exchange, Roger and I rolled a goat cart filled with enemy bodies and tossed it on its side to make a barricade, which we fortified by blowing a small avalanche of boulders, effectively blocking the road from below.

They will not be able to rush us with whatever vehicles they have. They'll have to come on foot, which unfortunately, they're more than glad to do for promises of eternity with virgins and other assorted heavenly privileges. From his perch, Roger will control the road. From my all too vulnerable position, I will spray the nearby hillsides he cannot fully control should the enemy approach that way.

There are a million ways this could go

wrong, but this is the best Roger and I can do. I've heard he's good, deadly good, and I hope to God he is, or else, we'll die and soon.

In my head I do one final accounting of all our provisions. I check off the 50 cal machine gun battery, the mound of grenades, and the two RPG launchers at my disposal, which I'm not expert or skilled at, but as I told Roger and as I hope, will be like "riding a bicycle" once my basic training comes back to me.

Did we miss anything? I go through it again, and all I come up with is my earlier conversation with Roger. Maybe I should have been more positive.

"We're not going to let them get to our team," I told him.

"No, ma'am."

"We're probably going to die tonight, but they will not get to them until we breathe our last breath and shoot our last bullet. You with me on this?"

"Yes, ma'am."

"We're up against it, soldier. This is going to turn ugly fast."

"Yes, ma'am. It's ugly enough already."

"No, soldier, it ain't. We ain't seen ugly yet."

He grinned at me. "They ain't seen our kind of ugly either."

I stared him down, and he stared right back.

I can still see his eyes now, intense, killer eyes. Do mine look like that? If not, they'll look like that soon enough, I suppose.

As dark reaches its blackest pitch, I hear them approach. Small engines, creaky suspensions—pickup trucks, it sounds like. Up above, from Roger's perch, I hear a single report. Down below I hear the sound of glass shattering and a second later a crash.

A second report follows, echoing off the cliff walls around us, and then, something explodes down below.

"Shot off one of their RPGs, right off that bastard's shoulder."

OK, so he's good, though I wish I weren't hearing this much glee in his voice.

Through my night vision goggles I see two figures hop over the barricade. Report, report. Down they go. Another is making the climb, but before he can make the top, report, falls backward.

Then, silence, the kind that lays heavy on you. The kind where only your heartbeat thumps in your ears. I'm scared.

"Stand by, ma'am. This is when they figure the road's a dead end and they have to get more creative."

Silence returns. Shadow spots them first, smells them, really, since he can't see them from his position. He barks. Their greenish silhouettes appear in my night vision field. Three of them.

I fire one short burst, followed by another. Two of them go down for sure, but the third? I can't tell if I got him.

"One's still crawling toward you, about thirty yards. Can't get him from here, but you can, with a grenade. Your eleven o'clock, thirty yards and closing. A close enough toss gets him."

Fears grips me as I grasp for the grenades. I grab one, take the pin out, toss it to my eleven o'clock. I barely close my eyes as it blows, and the flash still blinds me a bit.

But I still see them, three more figures, now crawling up from an incline slightly below the road.

Burst, burst. Check. Burst.

"I think I got 'em all," I say, my voice raspy and breathless.

"Can confirm. Blew one, shot three." He pauses. "All clear for now. Doing good, ma'am. Six KIA for you to my five."

"Let's stay focused," I say, my voice strains for composure, even if my head spins at the thought.

I've never killed before.

Until now I've rested in the fact that my job, spotting bombs and finding injured or missing people, saves lives. I resist the heaving impulse to throw up what little food I've consumed in the last twelve hours. They're over there, I'm over here. I can't see them. For the moment, that's all that gets me through, except I would like to remember how many people I've saved. It's gotta be more than six, right?

Well, there's twelve at my back right now,

moaning and bleeding out. They'll have to do for the moment.

"Anything?" I ask.

"Quiet."

"You think that's all of them?"

"Nah. You can always count on more cockroaches crawling up."

Cockroaches, that's how he gets through it. To Roger, they ain't more than cockroaches. That's how he keeps his balance positive.

At that moment I hear a woosh.

"Incoming!" Roger yells in my ear.

But I don't close my eyes, and out there, beyond the barricade, a big orange flash goes up followed by a second. I don't see anything else. I'm blinded, thanks to my night vision goggles not being up to snuff, not self-regulating like they're supposed to, because no one gave me another pair when I complained, since a dog handler doesn't see this kind of action, right? And if she does, she's cowering behind some rock with her dog while the real tough necks take care of business.

Net, net, I'm blind. I'm hopeless.

"Helo, ours," Roger says in my ear.

Down below I hear more explosions. I take off the goggles and close my eyes tight shut, hoping that will help them come back quicker. When I open them again, I see a blur, swinging to my left, a tether, and hanging from it, the help we never thought would come our way.

Pain bites at my side. I reach for it. My hand comes back moist and red.

Here in Colorado, on the land I shouldn't have to protect, and with only a data disc to guard at my back, I don't believe the helicopter I hear above will bring help. Quite the opposite. Here my buddies are now my enemies. And the reason for my stand boils down to my own pride and anger.

I rock on my chair, not so much to keep myself awake, but to fidget away my fear.

I'm not blinded by a flash, but by a bright light from the aircraft. I could shoot it if I wanted, but I won't. No, there will only be one dead body tonight. Mine.

This is why I sit fully exposed on this porch where people are supposed to sip lemonade, read a magazine, or do some knitting. But this night, you will paint a laser dot on my forehead and take me out. Go ahead, boys. Kill your hero. End her misery, please. Be afraid of her. She's a killer, a mangled one, but you better believe she'll do it again if you don't fix her for good, right now.

I keep rocking. Through a blurred sheet of tears I see it, a tether swinging down to the front yard. He's bigger than I expect for a commando doing this job. He's holding something white, a flag. Before I can discern what that means, he falls like a lump on the ground. Dust kicks up around him into a haze of white light. He stumbles to get up.

He stands there, holding a white flag. It and his loose shirt billow in the downdraft.

He's yelling something I can't hear.

I rock and rock in my chair.

"Jane," I hear finally as the helicopter rises into the black sky. "It's me, Dan."

He walks closer, stops, takes a few more steps. I see him eyeing me and the dogs. Yeah, the dogs, I should command them to attack, but I won't.

Shady whines, perhaps asking what to do, perhaps tired of my madness.

Dan comes closer, still calling out my name. He's now standing right below the porch's edge. He hesitates, then climbs into the planter below, and puts his hand on the wood deck.

"Jane, please. Do you know what time it is?"

"Not Miller time, I take it?"

He smiles at that. "I wish." He grows serious again. "It's 3 AM. They've been trying to get your attention for hours."

"And they finally decided to send you in."

"Please, Jane. Can we end this?"

"Do you even know what this is, big boy?"

"OK, tell me."

"You and I made a deal with the Devil, and now there's hell to pay."

"What do you mean?"

"Brady. We should've never let him go. We should have given him my fancy legs, yank out whatever's ticking inside Shadow's hip, let everybody know I's gang-raped, and that's how I blew my legs out from under me. Because I was too weak to take it and pay attention to where I was stepping."

"Jane, that's—"

"Crazy?"

"No one's going to think that."

"Well, at least they can have their damn legs back." Weeping, I reach down and roll up my pants. Roughly and without the usual care, I rip off the bindings, slide off one leg, and I toss it out to the yard. I do the same with the other.

That's when I notice it. Dan standing tall arms up to paint a Y, my big boy human shield. His eyes are looking with horror at my face, where I'm guessing a red dot is dancing along my forehead.

"It's OK, Dan, let 'em do it."

"No!" He jumps up, kicking the shot guns aside and swiping the rifle off my lap. He reaches over me, and he covers me with that thick body of his. "No!" he shouts again.

With both hands I grip and pull his shirt. I

stuff my face into it, and I cry, remembering that tears and crying, that's how springs of hope bust through.

Chapter 7

The walls in this room are white, not quite as snow, but near it, just like the other room, the one with a bed and a portable urinal where I've slept the last, what? Two, three days? Who knows? I sit at a chair I don't feel under me, a wheelchair, to be precise. I float when they roll me along. I hover now that I'm facing her.

I know her, I think. Her face seems familiar, and finally through the fog and haze, my mind connects her to something in my recent past. My arrangement, maybe? Yes, she's the one I've visited every week for the past six months, except when by special dispensation, such as when on travel for one of my jobs. But what is her name? I can't place it. The fog is too dense around the place where her name labels her face, her thin face, capped up top by a bowl of brassy hair.

"Are you going to say anything, Jane?" she asks.

"What's your name?" I ask, feeling the words roll out on my tongue thick and round.

"Martha. You don't remember who I am?"

"I remember you, just not your name. Martha, you said?"

"Yes."

"You wasn't with Jesus, was you?"

She smiles. "No, but someone else by the same name was. That's good. Good that you remember that. Where did you learn it?"

"I don't know... Oh, wait. There was this thick book, with pictures, and Papa read it to me, at night, before I went to bed. Not in bed, though, as he didn't want me to fall asleep during the Lord's stories. That's what the book was called, you know. The Lord's stories."

"Do you remember what Martha did?"

I shake my finger. "She got upset with Mary. Because Mary wasn't doing what she was supposed to. Or that's what Martha thought, but Jesus, he wasn't having none of it. He scolded Martha. Because Mary had chosen the right thing."

"And what was that?"

I rub my eyes and shut them tight. "You ask a lot of questions. Why do you do that? Is that what Jesus would have you do to me?"

She considers my question, gives me a non-answer. "We're going to adjust your dosage."

"Huh?"

"Your medicine."

"Oh. Am I sick? I don't feel sick, just like I woke up but my lungs ain't breathing full yet."

"That will wear off."

I open my eyes, and I'm looking at my legs, or more like it, my thighs. "What happened to my legs? I can't feel them. And they seem short. Is that the medicine doing that?"

She doesn't answer right away, and I have to look up to her before she says, "No, it's not the medicine. But you're doing better. Much better. How about we take you back to your room for a little more rest, and then we'll talk again."

"Alright," I say, my tongue feeling thicker and drier now.

As they wheel me out I hear her saying something hushed and terse to one of the women in the white coats. I look down at my legs, and I can feel them, but only in part. Just under my thighs, but not under my knees. I try to lift one of them so I can see all the way down to my foot. It doesn't work, so I try the other.

That's when I start screaming that someone's cut off my legs. They did it here, I'm sure of it, so I yell at the top of my lungs every curse I can pull out of the fog until they give me something sharp in my arm, and the fog drowns me all the way again.

The light comes in yellow and warm through a window too far up for me to reach. I'm in my room again, in my bed. The fog is gone, but my stomach churns something fierce. I feel dizzy, so I lay down again.

I'm alone in here, in this cold white room

that makes me think of winter and snow shoes in the Colorado high country. How I wish I were out again, a dog at my side, snow all around, a cold wind chaffing at my face. The pure, thin air out there—I long for it in place of the stifled, dense sanitized fumes in here.

Glad I don't drift in fog anymore, part of me wishes for it. I know about my legs now, what happened to them. It hurts to know. Now that my head sees clear and starts to recall, I can't face it all, not at once, so yes, give me a little more fog, please, or a lot, and just leave me in there.

"How are you feeling, Jane?" she asks.

I see her now, standing over the foot of my bed, holding a clipboard in her hand. "I'm feeling. I guess that's the best I can tell you."

"You remember my name?"

"Martha."

"You remember us talking about Martha?"

"Yes, just a few minutes ago, right?"

"Yesterday," she says. And I guess the fog was stronger and lasted longer than I thought.

"Do you know why you're here, Jane?"

"Because I want to die."

She pauses there, just long enough to give me the impression I've surprised her. "Do you still want to die?"

"No. No one wants to die. But sometimes wanting to live is harder."

"How so?"

"Because it hurts. The pain grabs you all the time. Whereas when you die, it's a one shot deal. Put you down, over and done. I guess a better way to say it is that it's easier to die than to live."

"Do you think living is only about pain?" she asks.

"Do you have proof to make me think otherwise? If so, I'd love to see it. I'd like for you to show me one day of my life where I didn't have to push through pain."

Martha pauses for a moment. "Do you remember your dogs?"

"Shadow and Shady."

"You're smiling. Why's that?"

"They're good dogs. Shady makes me smile plenty. She's a character, frustrates me and makes me laugh with her antics all at once."

"Would you say she gives you pain, when she frustrates you, I mean?"

"In a manner of speaking, I reckon so. But she makes up for it."

"How so?"

"She loves me."

"What about Shadow? Does he love you?"

"He does. In his own way, though. He's more reserved. But he'd die for me. Not sure Shady would do that, but he would." I point to my face and shut one eye. "That's why he lost his one eye and messed up the other. He was dying for someone else, but he didn't in the end."

"So he went through some pain, too."

My eyes tear up. "I reckon he did endure a lot more than some. More than his fair share, for sure."

"Do you think he wants to die?"

"What are you saying now? That I have less gumption than a dog?"

She doesn't reply, lets the silence suck me along to say more.

"Well, let me tell you. He's a dog, but he's better than most people I know. Stronger, too."

"Stronger than you?"

"Yeah, maybe."

"What would it do to him if you died?" she asks.

"He'd be done. He'd wanna die too."

"You sure?"

"Bring him. Ask him."

"Dogs don't talk."

"That they don't. But they do communicate. You just don't know how. You never will because for you it's all about talking and asking clever questions. You think that's how you get to truth. But it ain't. No one answer and no one hundred or one million answers will give you truth."

"How do you get the truth, then?"

"Weren't we talking about Jesus a few minutes ago? See what he has to say on the subject."

"Tell me," she says.

"That would be an answer. And what did I just tell you about answers?"

She excuses herself. Through the door I can hear her saying something to the nurse in the white coat. It sounds harsh again, something about my medication.

When I wake up, Martha is there again. Next to my bed I see a wheelchair, and propped on it, my prosthetic legs.

"Good morning," she says. "It's a beautiful day outside. I thought we'd go for a walk."

I turn my face away from the wheelchair and face the wall next to my bed. As I shift my weight, I feel an ache in my hips and back. Pain I ain't felt for some time. Not since the first time I strapped on and started using them legs.

"I can't walk," I say.

"Sure, you can. I've seen you. You walk very well, in fact."

"With those things."

"Yes. After all your physical therapy, you learned—"

"I know what I went through. I was there.

You don't have to remind me."

"So let's go for a walk, then."

"Not on those things."

"Why not?"

"They're the reason I'm here. If they haven't told you, then they lied to you, or they're not giving you all the facts for your precious analysis."

"I don't understand."

"Or you don't want to understand is more like it. Get it clear in your head. I ain't putting on no fake legs. Period."

"OK, then perhaps we can go in the wheelchair. I'll take you. The air is crisp outside."

"Leave me alone," I say. "Leave me the hell alone. And in case you're wondering, it ain't the meds anymore. This is me. All me. One hundred percent. The piece of crap that's left. If you can't deal with it, then you best pump me with some more of them psychedelics of yours."

Chapter 8

Martha gives it a few minutes, asks me a few more questions, and when I don't reply, she leaves. Tired of staring at the white wall, I turn to the other side. The wheelchair and legs are gone. The pain in my hips and lower back remains.

On my nightstand, I see a single book. I have this book at home. When I open it, I see it's my book, signed inside by Cassandra Godinez.

The book talks about the Pacific Crest Trail, everything you want to know about it, whether you want to do it all the way from the Mexico to the Canada border, or in short stretches. I love this book. I love the dreams it puts in my heart. I love its photos of a country so big and varied, from hot, sandy desert with tumble weeds that will bowl you over, to snowy mountain peaks and passes that will give you headaches for lack of oxygen.

I want to do it someday, the whole thing. I told Cassandra, and she got me the book. Except I need legs for that, don't I?

The thought makes me want to put the book down, but the pretty pictures of California, Oregon and Washington State vistas keep me glued to it. The images of raw country make me think of a time when this land lay mostly pristine and untouched, unscarred by highways, unspoiled by smoke stacks and refuse, and unmarred by the cruelty and outright savagery of the man who would seek to conquer it.

"Thems're hefty thoughts," I whisper to myself with a bitter grin.

My eyes fill up with tears. I wonder whether the springs of hope threaten to bust open because I'm feeling sorry for myself again, or because of the pretty pictures that beckon me to the great outdoors. One thought bubbles up and floats above all others in my confused mind: this is silly, ain't it? Me lying in this bed because, basically and at the core of it all, I'm feeling sorry for myself. Having a little girl's pity party, my own red-faced tantrum. Refusing to put on them legs because I've shown their owners my disdain, and stubbornness says, hell, no, you can't put those on.

I lay the book on my stomach and close my eyes.

They win, they that out of all the books put this one here. They win, the string pullers who always know how to tug at my heart to make me do what they want. They win, the ones that care about me or do such a good job pretending they do, whether or not I can tell the difference or whether their gestures of kindness, true or false, help me or not.

Well, I do know of at least two that care for me after their own way. They're out there, not mourning my absence, I hope, but running through fields of dry grass or along paths that will soon powder over with snow. They wait for me on a front porch, I hope, and not in some cage. They expect my return sitting up, ears at the ready, snouts searching the cool fall winds for my scent. Though one of them has undergone failure and rejection like I have, and though the other has witnessed horror and experienced physical loss in his own body, they ain't giving up. Not on this world, not on its challenges, and most of all, not on me.

For them, if nothing else, I need to get myself together, put on them legs or some other legs if I have to, and get the hell out of this place. Even if it's just for another eight to ten years before the dogs abandon me through death, I need to do this. I need to get up. I need to move.

I repeat that over and over. For them, if nothing else. I mouth it, staring up at the white ceiling beyond which I hope there truly is someone who can hear this twisted prayer of mine. For them, if nothing else, I say over and over again, and that desire to be there for two dogs and do right by them begins to feel like the only strength that makes sense, the only one I need to get out of this senseless, oppressive state. For them, if nothing else, I whisper hoping against hope that there is something else, someone else who will carry me beyond the day and time when caring for two dogs ain't enough or ceases to seem worthy or cuts out when death takes them away from me.

For them, if nothing else. After praying it for I don't know how long, the room's door clicks open with an answer of sorts.

Two familiar figures step in, Dr. Martha trailing a few steps behind them and closing the door to stand right by it.

"Hey, Jane," Allison says. "Look who wanted to see you." She's holding Rover, who squirming in her arms, is not being his usual calm self. "Look at him, hardly able to control himself."

I stretch out my arms and she brings him over to me, sets him on my stomach. His tiny paws dig into me and I groan. But as I hold him back from licking my face off, I notice I'm smiling.

"You turning into a therapy dog now, boy?" I ask him, and that riles him up some more.

"Easy, boy," I say, and he stands still though his whole body trembles. "Don't go peeing on these fine white linens now."

I pull him toward me and let him lick away. When he slows down a bit, I push him away, just far enough to look into those brown eyes. I expect to see that same sadness I saw in there before, but instead I find determination. Get out of that bed, he's telling me. I don't belong there. He's seen terrible things, too, and he ain't giving up. I shouldn't dare give up on him, either.

I look over at Allison. She's smiling back, the mirror of my face, I'm hoping. Over her left shoulder, a step behind, I see Cassandra's face. She's smiling, too, but hers is a more tentative expression. I notice they're both dressed in sport bras and running shorts. I trace down their bare legs, and sure enough, I find running shoes there.

"Saturday?" I ask.

"Mmm, Sunday, actually," Allison replies. "Still, Cassandra and I decided to make it long run day."

"What are you doing going out for a long run?" I ask Allison.

Her lips twist into a grin. "I decided to run it with you. The marathon. I'm all signed up, so I'm committed now."

"A little late to start training, ain't it?"

"I'm up to eight miles," she says. "That's good, right?"

She's asking for trouble, I don't have the heart to tell her. "Well, I reckon I've lost a couple of runs myself, so I'm not much better off than you."

Cassandra looks over at the doctor, then back at me. "Just two Saturdays," she tells me.

"Two Saturdays?" I sit up, and groan again when that causes Rover's paws to dig into my belly again. "How long have I been in here?"

Allison takes Rover from me and steps back. "As long as it takes. It doesn't much matter, does it?"

"Ten days," Cassandra says, again stealing another glance back at Martha, like the length of my stay here is a sensitive subject.

"Ten days," I echo back. "Yeah, I suppose I

did need it."

"You're feeling better?" Allison asks. "Maybe up for a walk or a little run? It's past noon, nice and warm out there."

My gaze lands on Cassandra again, and I notice the bag she's holding in her hand.

"Your running outfit," she says.

"I guess I'll need me some legs if we're going to make it work," I say, now aiming my gaze at Dr. Martha.

"If you're up to it," she says. I hear caution in her voice, the sort that comes from seeing her fair share of the sort of emotional seesawing patients like me go through.

"Won't know if I don't try, will I?" I reply.

She smiles and nods before she steps out of the room. At once Cassandra and Allison step up and crowd me.

"You sure you want to do this?" Allison whispers. "You don't have to do it if you don't want to."

"Why, because them legs are evil?" I ask her with none of her care not to have my words recorded by listening devices.

"Let's talk outside," Cassandra whispers. She hands me my GPS watch. "Neat gadget," she notes in her full voice. "I used it yesterday to clock the walking track around this place. One mile on the nose, even after averaging several laps. It might get a little repetitive, but sixteen of those gets us our mileage for today."

"And lots of time to talk," I add.

"And that," Cassandra says with a raised eyebrow. "We'll run at a *conversational* pace, like we're supposed to."

The door opens and Martha rolls in the wheelchair with the two prosthetic legs. I take a good look at them to certify that, yes, they're my better set of legs, the ones I use for hiking and other strenuous jobs.

"Alrighty, then," I say. "Let's do this."

Though they offer to wheel me out, I opt to walk on my own. The first few steps down the long, wide tiled corridor feel odd, reminiscent of times not long ago when I learned to walk again. Maybe it's the residue drugs in my system that throw off my balance, I tell myself. Regardless, by the time I reach the end of the corridor, I'm feeling more like myself. My body readjusts, though I can't shake the feeling that it's my mechanical ankles and knee braces that are adjusting, adapting, self-calibrating as it were.

The air outside is crisp. Though the sun shines unhindered by a few rolling white clouds, it feels like definite fall, here in the middle of October. Or more like the end of it, I remind myself, having lost nearly two weeks of my life in this place.

Allison ties Rover's leash to a pole in the shade, a water bowl already set there for his comfort and enjoyment. That's when I see them: Shady and Shadow. They don't welcome me with Rover's earlier shaky mess, but their faces are fixed on me like there's nothing else in the world. They sit at attention, but I know inside they want to pounce on me.

"*Hierr*," I say, bending down, and they both strain at the end of their leashes to get to me. I allow a few moments of horsing around, and then I tell them to sit. The calm allows me to hand Shady's leash to Cassandra while I take Shadow's.

"I can take him," Allison offers.

"He won't knock me down," I tell her.

We start down the first stretch along a rubber composite track that feels firm, yet spongy enough to provide a gentle running surface. Cassandra and Allison make idle chat for most of the first lap while I make no sound other than that of my breathing.

With about a tenth of a mile to go, we take our first walk break.

"How's the case going?"

Both of them seem to hesitate. Allison takes the lead with, "Let's not talk about that."

"There's been more bombings, I take it?"

"One more in Phoenix," Cassandra says. "Case is cold as ice. But that's all we're going to say, and you don't need to be concerned over it. You did your part. They can do the rest."

I nod, remembering Dan's shirt and how I held onto it. "How's Dan doing?"

"Sends his regards," Cassandra says.

"Giving me that public affairs treatment, huh?" I ask her.

"Time to run," she says, and we end our walk break.

Though we're clipping a nice thirteen minute pace, I'm a bit out of breath, way more than my usual. I tally that up to the drugs and complete inactivity for ten days. Still, as we finish our second mile and stop at a water fountain to drink, my lungs start to open up to fill up wider and capture more of the crisp Colorado air.

"Where's this place, anyway?" I ask.

"Right here in Fort Collins," Allison says. "Not far from the University."

"When are they letting me out?"

She points down at my legs. "Now that those are on, tomorrow, if you'd like. Maybe today."

"That what Martha said?"

"That's what she'll say when I'm through talking with her," Allison replies.

With a grin, I look over at Cassandra. "So

let's plan for another ten days."

"Oh, God, I hope not," she says. "This place needs to fade small into your rear view mirror, soonest and faster."

We start running again, mostly in silence now. Though the air is cool, we're starting to sweat. Well, Allison and I are. Cassandra and the dogs are doing fine.

We complete three, four, five laps, and soon Allison starts struggling. Up to now she's done her runs in the morning, she huff-says, and the warmer setting is bringing her down. I tell her this is good training, that it will toughen her up, especially since for us slow runners, we'll be finishing the marathon well into late morning or early afternoon.

As best she can, she gives me a sideways smile and breathes out, "Thanks."

I dwell on her smile with one of my own. For once I'm the one spurring on someone else. The thought feels good, even alongside the shameful debris that yet another break and one more hospitalization bring.

As we reach the eight mile mark, we stop for

a water break at the fountain, and though I want to remain encouraging, I'm wondering whether we should tell Allison to call it quits. Her face is bright red, and she can scarcely get her breath.

She catches my eye. "I'm slowing you down. You guys go ahead, maybe I'll walk."

I know Cassandra will want to push on, at our pace, but I say, "We'll walk with you."

"Nah, I don't want to mess up your training."

"We're doing this together, right?" I ask her. She nods.

I pat her on the shoulder. "We stick together. We get each other through."

We walk a ways, roughly one half of the next mile. Above us thin clouds drift from the west, soon thickening up a bit. From time they cover the sun, in part or in full, and with the passing of the afternoon leading into evening, the air around us cools further.

At about the three quarter mark for this mile I say, "Let's see if we got our second wind."

We start trotting again, slow this time, we

make it to the nine mile marker and keep going. Our walk breaks now come by feel rather than at set distances. As I tell Allison, "we're managing it now." Really I ought'a say, surviving it, but that would come across too negative. In this managing mode, we pass miles ten, eleven, twelve, and as we start on thirteen, I say I'm beat and we'll call it a day at a half marathon.

To her credit, Cassandra who though not looking so fresh anymore seems like she could go another five, well, she doesn't say a thing. Though she usually would play the role of taskmaster, this time I think she's glad to have me out of that room. From the way she smiles as we come to a stop, I'm guessing there's more to it.

"Now you have a choice," Cassandra says. "You can shower here, or you can shower at home."

"My home?"

"The one and only."

I stop, trading looks between Allison as she sucks water from the fountain and Cassandra as she stands there smirking at me.

"Yeah, that means what you think it means," Cassandra says. "Allison won't be needing to do any of her persuasive talking. Deal was if you got out on your legs you could go home, and you overachieved by some."

Even though I see it through a now vanished drug induced fog, I recall the last shower I had here. They carted me in on a wheelchair and hosed me off, is what they did. Choosing the sitting bull act back in my own tub seems like a dream by comparison. Yet, for a few moments I go back and forth. Am I ready to rejoin my real world? Do I want to?

Chapter 9

Allison insists I ride with her, says her car is more comfortable than my 4Runner, which Cassandra drove here in order to pack the dogs. I take Rover with me, though. I hate it when celebrities do it, but I set him on my lap and curl two fingers through his collar. With my other hand I cup his chest. He ain't going anywhere I ain't.

"You like him, don't you?" Allison asks me as we pull out of the parking lot.

"Better than you, I reckon."

"What makes you say that?"

"The face you made when you first saw him."

"I made a face?"

"Sure did. And on the drive up from Denver

I was kind'a thinking you and he might make a good pair."

"They had a dog just like him in that show Frazier," Allison explains. "I didn't like that show. You've seen it, right? In reruns on the local channel 5?"

"Can't say that I have."

She shakes her head, at least this once restraining her usual diatribe about my cultural turpitude. Yup, she actually called it that once, obviously because she thinks that last word sounds cool more than she knows what it means.

"Jane, can I ask you something? And you tell me if this isn't a good time, OK?"

"Sure."

"Remember how we used to talk about me and you going into business? Maybe turning that barn your father built but never used into an office and—"

"I remember," I say, picturing in my head the rust-brown barn that stands about a mile south of the ranch house, the dirt trail that feeds to it overgrown with bushes and prairie grass.

"Well, with what's happened. It's caused me to rethink things. I think that was a really good idea then, and I don't know why we dropped it. Maybe things got weird between us? But we're good friends now, aren't we?"

"I reckon we are."

"I think I can turn that loft into an apartment for me. There's a bathroom on the bottom floor, and it's got running electricity, right?"

"It'll be bitter cold in winter," I point out. "I think that's why we stopped talking about it."

She bites her lip. "My boyfriend says he can build up some walls in the loft, insulate the floor and walls, and let a space heater do the rest. The space is small enough to make it work, don't you think?"

"I suppose it might."

"And at night, I'd pitch in. I can cook some nights, help around the house, whatever you need. I'll earn my keep. Then I go back to the barn and give you your privacy."

"Always nice to have a spare pair of hands around," I say. "Especially when I finally get going on my dog breeding and training business."

"You think we could do it, then?"

"Can I sleep on it?" I ask.

"Sure," she says, her voice ringing out with a hint of urgency.

And I know why. After what's happened, she wants to be close to me. She doesn't trust the other people in my life, namely the one that's been staying with me. But perhaps, most of all, she doesn't trust me.

"You and Cassandra bonded over the last few days?" I ask.

"Yeah. She's very nice." Allison taps me on the forearm to get my attention. Out of view from the outside, she gives me a sideways thumb sign, followed by a turn into a thumbs down. "She really cares for you," she adds to punctuate her point in reverse.

"Good. That would be one area of concern, three women in such proximity and all." I search for what to say next. "She's kind of a holy roller, you know that, right? *Penti-costal*."

Allison smiles at the way I'm playing along.

"I know. We've had quite a few *talks* about eternity and salvation over the last couple of days."

"She mostly keeps to herself, though. Only talks about that stuff if you want her to. Otherwise, she lets it drop."

"Yeah, I brought up going to church with you on occasion. So I guess that brought it on."

"Alright. So that wouldn't be an issue, then."

"I don't think so," Allison replies.

"I suppose the Christian thing to do would be to bring it up with her. It's ultimately my property and my decision, but I'll take her view into consideration."

"Sure."

"OK, like I said. I'll mull it over. Maybe your boyfriend can come by, check out the place, and explain to me what he'd recommend." Now it's me doing the tapping on the forearm to show her a thumbs up. "That'll help me decide, too."

She smiles back. "Thank you for being open to this. And yeah, think it through. It's your land, your property."

We drive in silence most of the way, except for me harassing Rover with questions about who asked my permission for him to come to my house. He looks up at me with his soulful brown eyes and licks me a couple of times. Sometimes a dog's answers prove themselves the simplest, most direct, and satisfying kind.

By the time Allison pulls up to the front of the house, Cassandra and the dogs are standing on the porch. Cassandra is holding a sign that reads "WELCOME HOME" in big purple letters. When I get closer I see that on one corner she's drawn two tiny purple hearts—a pretty good likeness if my art appreciation can render such judgments.

I smile at her, choosing to ignore the symbolism that points to my refusal to accept being pinned with that medal and her encouragement over the past couple of months to get over whatever's stopping me from receiving the honor.

Allison gets ready to go home for a shower before she runs back to cook me dinner with groceries she's bought for the occasion.

"Sounds great," I say. "Why don't you bring a change of clothes and an overnight bag while you're at it. Let's make a slumber party of it." With Cassandra at my back, I shoot Allison a wink.

"Great!" she says.

"After I get out of the shower, I'll go digging through the basement for a nice bottle of wine." I wink again. "Maybe two, if we can get Cassandra to try it and she gets to liking it."

Allison laughs and gets into her car to drive off.

As I walk into the house, Cassandra says, "Dan would like to talk to you, via video telecon. If you're up to it."

I stop and without turning to her, I say, "Let me see how I feel after the shower."

As I start moving forward again, Cassandra stops me with, "About the wine..."

"What about it?"

"Maybe it's not such a good idea this soon."

"Good point. I'll let you drink my portion."

Allison comes back ninety minutes later carrying a pan covered with aluminum foil that tells tales of a garlic eruption. She explains a Cuban co-worker gave her a jar of this marinade, something she pronounces *Moh-ho*. She's used it on a pork loin which she now plans to stick into my oven.

"That's gonna save me a lot of money on pest control," I'm telling her as she gets it going.

"Or the opposite if all the *cucarachas* from the Caribbean come flying in," Cassandra throws in, and the two of us have a laugh at that while Allison shakes her head and smiles.

She's a girl with a plan and on a mission to execute it. In another minute she's got white rice going on a pan while on another she sautés a mix of olive oil, chopped onions, green bell peppers, olives, and—you guessed it—more garlic! While that concoction hisses in the pan, she gets out a large can of black beans.

"Oh, that's gonna cause fumigation of a different kind," I say, and now the three of us laugh at my slightly more sophisticated than boy humor.

When we're done with the hazing, I go over to Allison and give her a big hug. I don't say it, but I appreciate that instead of mailing it home, she's trying something new, something special for me.

As if reading my mind, when I let her go, she says, "I hope it turns out OK." She adds that the pork will take another fifty minutes.

That leaves plenty of time for me to touch base with Dan. Do I want to do that? I weigh that one more time, like I did the whole time I was bathing.

I turn to Cassandra, and she knows without my saying a word to go set it up.

"You look good," Dan says from the laptop screen.

"A lot better without the M-16 and shotguns, huh?"

"You know what I mean."

"I feel good. Did a thirteen miler today."

"Yeah, Cassandra texted me. Good for you. You'll be ready for that marathon in no time."

He's being far too kind. With less than a month to go, I should have at least a twenty miler under my belt by now. At least that's what all the websites and the book Cassandra gave me say.

"It'll be a death march, no doubt," I say. "Without the funeral at the end, I hope."

"Well, I just wanted to welcome you home. Even if I'm not there myself." He pauses. "Anyway, you're probably tired, and Cassandra tells me it's near dinner time. I best let you go."

"That busy, huh?"

His grin tells me he knows I mean him. "Yeah, you can say that."

"How are things going? Any breaks in the case?"

He hesitates. "I really rather not say."

"I'm not going to crack, Dan."

He hesitates again because the natural thing to say here is that, yes, actually, he has every reason to believe I will crack. After all, he saw it first hand, didn't he? Me cracking like a thousand eggs tossed from a skyscraper.

"You really shouldn't worry yourself with this stuff, Jane. Trust me, there's nothing you can do about it. I'm beginning to think that holds for me, too."

"You can trust me on this: I don't wanna do nothing about it. But you sound like you're gasping under a ton of bricks. You can lay it on me. I won't break."

He thinks about that for a moment. "You were right. About them infiltrating, like they did back in Iraq. I pulled those cases, compared them to the situation here. Found several instances of people being blackmailed into blowing themselves up."

"But no one will listen." Hence the ton of bricks on him, I don't add.

"I'm straining my persuasive powers."

"So you found the same M.O. in that Phoenix explosion."

He waves his hands. "OK, I appreciate you wanting to hear me out and all that. But you don't need this. And I'll be straight-up here.

Yes, because I don't think you're ready. Because I think you need some time to think about stuff other than this."

His sudden outburst shocks me. My natural reaction here, and the one I'm millimeters from unleashing, calls for lobbing a couple of acid bombs his way. But something holds me back. Something tells me to accept the way he's caring for me, and that same something recommends I need to do that more often from now on.

"Fair enough," I say. "Promise you won't work too late tonight."

"I don't make promises I can't keep," he replies with a gentle smile.

"Alright, then try drinking ten beers instead."

He laughs at that, and I like the way his voice sounds now as he laughs, even garbled through the Internet connection. More than that I like how I made it sound that way.

"Hey, Jane," he says before we end the connection. "Give Cassandra a break. She's on your side. I wouldn't have known what was going on with you that night, except she called me. When I got there, she was screaming up a bloody storm to stop them from going in heavy on you."

"I didn't see her dropping out of no helicopter," I shoot back.

"If it hadn't been for her I wouldn't have been there in the first place. If she hadn't backed me up when I argued they should send me in, I wouldn't have been in that helicopter."

For an instant I'm gripping his shirt and crying into it again. I come out of it tense and sullen. "Thanks. I'll keep that in mind."

"She told you she's on leave, right?"

"Not really."

"For insubordination, and probably for threatening to blow the lid on how out of pocket and jurisdiction your buddies were. Among other things. You get what I'm saying, Jane?"

"Yeah, I suppose."

"She stuck her neck out for you, all those hours you were sitting on that porch. And now she's paying for it, and she's not done paying."

I look over my shoulder and into the kitchen. In there I can see Allison and Cassandra carrying on, laughing at each other's whatevers, and I wonder which of them is putting on the biggest act.

I don't have any explanation for it other than the garlic fumes, but Cassandra gives in. She has some wine. She starts with a small portion, measured as one of my fingers, thick as it is. She follows that with another, and another, plus one more, and so on, until soon, she's sitting there with her second half-full glass, sloshing it around as Allison showed her in order to "open it up." By this point, we're on bottle number 2, with Allison and Cassandra as the chief consumers thus far, as I'm still babying the last swig of my first modest pour.

With words that roll on her tongue as if flowing through thick syrup, Cassandra says to Allison, "You make some awesome Cuban porch shops."

"Why thank you," Allison replies, failing to mention this is the third time Cassandra makes the same statement. Perhaps I am the only one sober enough to do simple math.

"Now you say you met him at work?" Cassandra slurs, again, covering already treaded ground.

"Yeah. He's a facilities guy. Works there three to four days per week." She turns to me. "He's the guy I told you about. The contractor?"

"Oh, yeah," I say, already feeling a little less sure about bringing this guy in to remodel my barn's loft.

"He's pretty smart." Allison taps on her temple with her index finger. "Works at the hospital just enough to cover his medical. Then he swings over to construction Thursday to Saturday, sometimes Sundays, too. Does mostly small remodeling jobs, you know, bathroom tiling, sinks, moving a wall. All on his own."

She's said all this trading looks between me and Cassandra, and she's doing it so quick, her eyes look like they'll start spinning in their sockets at any moment.

"Now, you said he's Cuban?" Cassandra says.

"Yes. Grew up in Miami, moved up here after high school. Lives on his own."

"Well, you're going to make him very happy. Cubans love their pork, and these chops are just awesome."

Alright, there it is. How do I end this looping record? Please, somebody tell me. But I don't stop it. I figure Allison's up to something, refreshing Cassandra's glass with sometimes as little as a drip from the bottle. For her part Cassandra's no longer noticing, in spite of earlier objections. She keeps sipping like she sees some line on the glass below which she must keep the wine's level.

As she continues to drink it becomes clear that among drunks Cassandra falls into the introspective, sullen category. This stands in contrast to Allison, whose clever, bubbly personality unleashes any sort of inhibition she might hold when sober.

"You got quiet all of the sudden," Allison

notes.

Cassandra shrugs and takes another sip from her glass.

Allison turns to me. "You haven't said much about what you and Dan talked about."

"Actually I haven't said anything. The pork chops, rice and black beans had me too occupied I guess."

"How's he?" Allison presses.

"Tired. Stressed. Too busy. And so on."

Cassandra shoots Allison a stern look, and Allison catches the meaning, which I'm guessing has something to do with not getting anywhere near the bombings and Dan's task force investigation in front of the big, crazy chick.

Allison smiles. Undeterred, she turns to me. "You two getting together soon?"

"Like I said. He's busy. And I'm recovering."

"I've always found boys help my recovery," Allison replies with an upraised wine glass. She turns to Cassandra. "You must love it, being in the Army—"

"Air Force," Cassandra corrects.

Allison waves her hand. "Same point. All those cute guys in uniform, easy to *recover*."

Cassandra answers with a scowl.

Allison looks back at me for support.

"What Cassandra is too kind to mention," I say, "is that all them boys ain't all that cute, and the ones that are ain't worth the trouble. Besides, last thing you want to do is fall in love with a guy, only so that both of you can become pen pals when they deploy you on opposite sides of God's earth. It's been done, but if you're smart, you avoid it."

"Sure, if you say so," Allison replies.

"And what's your sudden interest with boys all of the sudden?" I ask her.

"All of the sudden?"

I shrug.

"Oh, you must have heard that at one time I played a wider field and thought I played a *different* field? That's incomplete information, I'm afraid." She takes a sip from her glass, her lips curled into a smile. "Rest assured, that was just a phase. I'm back to *normal* now."

That sets me back a bit. To try and shake off the effects of that mild stun grenade, I turn to Cassandra.

"How's things at the base these days?" I ask her.

"Haven't been there." She pauses to swirl the wine in her glass. "I've been taking some leave."

"Didn't know you had any planned."

"Of course I didn't."

Allison has to jump in. "She's been looking after you, silly."

And she could have done that while still doing her job at the base, even if part time. But that ain't her job, going to the base and going through the motions with the couple of mutts they have there. She should be down in Lackland doing real training with real dogs. Instead she's stuck with me, making sure I don't go off the rails and that I keep the government's investment secure.

"Dan told me," I say to Cassandra. "Is it true?"

Cassandra shakes her head.

"What?" Allison asks. "What's true?"

"That her leave ain't voluntary. That she's taking it on the chin on account of me."

"Is that true, Cassandra?" Allison asks, her voice registering concern that sounds almost cheery. She turns to me. "What else did Dan say?"

"I think we should let Cassandra tell the tale," I say. "Horse's mouth and all that."

"Yeah, I called him," Cassandra replies. "You want to make something of that, go ahead. So sorry for getting in your business. So sorry I didn't let them put one between your eyes like you were egging them to do."

Cassandra stands up and glass in hand goes over to the sink, where she dumps the wine. Her lips are twitching when she turns to me. She clenches her jaw, and it goes almost square. Her eyes are firing at me the way eyes do when anger wants to melt into tears but you won't let it.

"You know, I've heard so many stories about you, about things you did, how great you are with the dogs, what you did with Shadow on your four tours. That's all they did when I was coming up, talk about Captain McMurtry and how we should all be like her. I bought into it."

"And now you know," I say.

She's been leaning against the counter, holding onto it with both hands. Now she points a finger at me to say, "You're not the only one that went through hell. I may have come back with both my legs, but I got my soul crushed over there, just like everybody else."

I nod, stare at my own wine glass, push it away though it begs me to down it. "I know that."

I lower my eyes, and we say nothing else.

Chapter 10

Though she usually beats me out of bed in the morning, Cassandra is not up when I walk into the kitchen. Fearing she's taken off, I look out through the kitchen window to see her car still there, under the shade of the large oak tree that stands against the main driveway.

On the counter, I find a hot, steaming pot of coffee waiting for me. I pour myself a cup, grab my cellphone off the charger and turn it on before I stuff it into my sweatshirt's right pocket.

Still, lying on the couch where she slept, Allison gives me a non-enthusiastic wave. Her disheveled, tired demeanor leads me to almost say she should have let me set her up in the small day bed in my office upstairs, but I know the couch is comfortable enough, especially for someone her size. No, her morning struggle has a lot more to do with the amount of wine she consumed while working to loosen Cassandra's tongue through her own drinking.

I am formulating a cynical quip relaying some of those thoughts when I notice what she's watching.

"A little early for vampire shows, ain't it?" I ask.

She shrugs. "Nothing else on."

"News must be pretty boring." I say this knowing with what relish she consumes TV and Internet news. As if to respond to this thought, she turns her cellphone face down in a way that suggests she's hiding something.

"Something wrong?" I ask.

Allison raises her coffee cup. "Getting over the hangover."

She's not leveling with me. I'm sure of it. I stand there for a second and decide I need some fresh air. There's plenty of it outside, so I find my way to the front porch.

Inside my pocket, my phone's buzzing up a

storm. I ignore it.

The thought that I shouldn't be out here hits me as soon as I drop into the rocker. The images start coming, one after the other, flashbacks of vehicles approaching over there beyond the fence, flashbacks of me sitting at a machine gun station, flashbacks of helicopter tethers, some over there, dropping into an Afghanistan mountain, one here dropping someone I know and should love.

I shut my eyes tight, opening them to the morning sunlight, seeing spots where a clear field of view should extend before me, blinded like I was that night. Hell, I think to myself. I'm having flashbacks inside flashbacks now. Just what I need.

Instinctively I reach for my right side, and I can feel it now like I felt it then, blood, fresh blood. Not the dried blood of those who I helped patch. My blood, I realize.

I shut my eyes again, demanding the memories leave me. My hand is still pressing against my right side when I reopen my eyes. Instead of blood, I feel my phone buzzing.

I take it out to see I have, among other things, a long stream of text messages from Candice, my agent. I skip to the last two.

"Lotta buzz this morning. Call me," the next to last one says, and the most recent contains a link along a note: "Need your help getting ahead of this."

I click on the link and it takes me to a tweet that says, "Why is Maj McMurtry left out of the investigation? Same reason she won't accept her two Purple Hearts? #wanttruth #coverup"

The message comes from someone named @artinErin. I click on her avatar to check out her profile. It reads: "One person's Conspiracy is another's Veracity." I nod to myself. Same crazy chick that's been harping about my heroism on one hand while on the other she denounces the government's mistreatment of me and wounded veterans. She's left me alone for a while, a testimony to our if-you-ignore-them-they-go-away strategy—well, my agent's strategy. From the sounds of it, though, and if I dare plow through all the text messages, Erin's back on crusade.

Last thing I need right now is a chat with my agent. Don't need no diatribes about how I've been neglecting my brand, how I can't hide in this day and age, how I'm a hero and need to start "projecting" like one.

I drop the phone onto the small table between my rocker and the next. It goes off the edge and goes down onto the deck with a thump. I mutter something unclean and scramble to pick it up, in the process spilling some of my coffee on my lap and nearly dumping myself into a heap and onto the deck.

Allison comes out to ask, "You OK?"

"Candice wants to give me another of her pep talks."

I pick up the phone and look up at her. For a moment, her expression reflects the reason for my agent's texting tornado, though in another second I'm wondering whether I'm reading something more severe.

Allison looks down and walks past me to sit on the other rocker.

"Something's going on," I say. "That's why you flipped the channel to that vampire show.

Big news, I take it? Another airport goes pow."

She shakes her head. "Miami International. Really bad. Biggest one yet."

"When?"

"Seven this morning, Eastern Time."

I check the time on my cellphone's screen: 8:30 AM here, two hour difference, Dan's been running for over three hours. On my cellphone screen I see something else, a news alert, and I don't need to look at it to know what it concerns. I click on it anyway.

The story says two bombers blew themselves and whoever they could take with them. Coordinated attack, they say, two different terminals, detonations within seconds of each other. As I scroll down skimming over the repetitive text, I find several links to related stories. One catches my attention. Titled "Where is Jane McMurtry," it stares me in the face.

"I'm right here," I mutter.

"What?" Allison asks.

I show her my phone's screen.

"Yeah," Allison notes. "Apparently some

bloggers are squawking about you being excluded from the investigation. 'Hasn't been seen in nearly two weeks,' they keep saying." She pauses. "They don't know where you were, so no worries there, OK?"

"If they find out—when they find out, I should say—there goes my brand, don't it?"

"People would understand."

"Would they? Or would they be more concerned with their own hides, like they always are?" I look her in the eye, sternly enough she looks away. "So are they talking about shutting down airports yet, until they sort all this out? You know that's going to cause a hell of a lot of *inconvenience*. That's when people will really get to caring."

Allison's chest rises and falls several times. She's taking deep breaths as if to exhale tension and inhale wise words she can lay on me.

"People know you deserve those two Purple Heart medals," she says finally.

"What does that have to—"

"You should accept them, Jane. You do deserve them."

"We've been over this—"

"Yeah, we have. And it still makes no sense. Yeah, I get that people died over there and you came home alive. I get that you are bitter about the way you lost your legs. I get that you want to show up your superiors with your defiance because you don't think they did right by you. But it's all missing the point from where I sit. Because that's not what the Purple Heart is about. And before you tell me I don't know what I'm talking about, I'll just say fine, I don't. But you do, Jane. You should know better."

I don't know what stuns me most, her assertive passion on this topic, setting aside her usual bubbly, happy-go-lucky self, or the fact that she knows more than she ought.

"What do you know about the way I lost my legs?" I ask her.

She freezes for a moment. "Dan told me."

Now I'm the one that looks away.

"There's no shame in that, Jane. You didn't rape yourself. In my book, if anything, it makes you more of a hero. Victimized twice in two very tragic ways. And look at what you've done since."

"Yeah, look at what I have done," I whisper.

"Oh, let me count the ways. Learned to walk again. Rescued two skiers from an avalanche. Helped solve a major criminal investigation so that kids don't keep going missing and families don't keep wondering if their kids are coming home tonight. And you've inspired people, Jane. So many people."

I raise my hand. "Please. Enough pep-talk."

"Well, how about this? You've inspired me. That's right. Me. I'm proud to be your friend."

When I turn to face her, she's reaching out her hand to me, palm up. I take it.

"Let us honor you like you deserve," she says.

"OK."

"OK, you'll do it?"

I grin at her. "Yeah, maybe."

Allison squeezes my hand and flashes a smile that comes across more like a grimace.

Our moment would last longer, but the screen door swings open and two German shepherds bound onto the porch. Shadow and

Shady stand at the top of the steps that lead down on to the yard, and Rover rolls out in a white blur to stand between them. All three of them stare to the east, more or less to the spot in the road where the gate now stands locked.

Shadow rumbles a low growl, and that moves Rover to let out a single shrieking bark.

I shield my eyes from the eastern sun and notice vehicles there, large ones, vans I determine through all my squinting.

Cassandra comes out, rubbing her eyes, a pair of binoculars in her hand. She hands them to me.

"News crews," she says. "I count three, not local."

"What?" I say.

"When are you planning to call your agent back?" Cassandra asks.

With a turn of the adjustment wheel, I sharpen the image in the binoculars and hear them whirring as the image stabilization kicks in. I count three news vans. When I scan farther up the road I see a plume of dust rising up behind a fourth as it approaches.

I sweep back to the ones by the gate, for now frozen there. I picture them staring at the hand-written sign that reads "TRESPASSERS WILL GET A GOOD CHEWIN', AND IF THAT DON'T SUFFICE, A SHOOTIN'."

"You really need to call her," Cassandra adds.

"I don't see as I do."

"Well, thank you for ignoring her," Cassandra adds. "Woke me up three times this morning with incoming calls."

I turn to face her. "Well, bed ain't the place to undo a hangover. Drink lots of water and coffee."

She squints, and though at first I think she's frowning at me, I realize a pulsing shot of her headache just hit her. Cassandra squints again when Shady lets out a couple of barks.

I turn back toward the road in time to see a figure climbing over the gate. Through the binoculars I make her out, and after the stabilization kicks in again, I'm sure.

I watch her make her way along the road. From time to time she looks our way and raises her arms, like she's surrendering to us. The inkling to go inside and grab a shotgun dissolves when I realize all my guns are now under lock and key somewhere, and I don't have the key nor know the somewhere.

"Can you tell who it is?" Allison asks.

I hand her the binoculars before I look down at my dogs, standing there like fully wound rubber bands, ready to snap should I tell them. I could. I'm well within my rights. Give the command and let them go rip her up. Though I consider that for more than a few seconds, I look up with a measure of shame that I did. Besides, it would make for nasty TV, the kind that's sure to kill my brand.

She's closer now, and as she approaches, she raises her arms more than before.

"Great," Cassandra says next to me now that recognition joins with anger. "Bridget Suarez."

"Well, we already got us four gals here," I say. "One more won't upset the balance too much."

Bridget stops when Shady and Rover bark at

her. She stands with arms raised. She's close enough that I can see her teeth through her forced smile.

"I was hoping we could talk again?" she says.

That sets off Rover, and he leaps the steps in one hop and races to encircle her with a white barking blur.

"Rover, come," I say in a firm voice.

He stops, looks up at me with brown eyes that question my wisdom.

"Come!"

He looks up at Bridget and growls before hop-trotting back to us.

"I know I'm trespassing, but I really hope we can talk."

"About what?" I ask.

"I spoke with your agent earlier. She should have set things up with you."

"Oh? Did you call her to confirm that?"

"I'm afraid I haven't been able to reach her."

I pull out my phone and scan through the text messages. Sure enough, one of them says I should meet with Bridget Suarez. It promises a puff-piece interview, like the one the other day. It's the way we get ahead of this, Candice promises. And oh, "great time to announce you're working on setting up a ceremony for the pinning of your Purple Heart medals!"

I look up at Bridget and say, "Come on up. I promise the dogs won't chew on you."

"Oh, good," she replies with a wide smile. "And I promise I won't report or ask you any questions about where you've been over the last ten days or why."

Chapter 11

Bridget and I are standing by the barn while her camera man makes square frames with his fingers to check how this or that other angle will work.

"I think this will turn into total awesomeness," the camera guy, Richard something-or-other says. "With this sweeteliscious light, that killer rust-brown barn just makes you two pop!"

Restraining the impulse to tell him I'll pop him one for being so California-peppy, I say, "Alright, you best go fetch your gear."

"And my assistant?"

"Sure."

He toe-leaps like a ballet dancer and prances off. That leaves Bridget and me alone. Against

Cassandra's better judgment, I insisted she take the dogs by the front gate to restrain the horde there while Cassandra gives them a pseudo news conference of her own choosing. In spite of my aversion to news watching, I make a mental note to catch some of that later, my little reward for what I have to endure here with Bridget.

Using my walkie talkie, dusted off for the occasion, I radio Cassandra to let her know Richard is coming and to, yes, let his assistant come back with him. No vehicles, though, as agreed, I say eyeing Bridget. I re-snap the radio onto my belt when we're done talking.

"How did you find out?" I ask her.

"About? I know so much, it's hard to keep it all straight."

"You said you knew where I was the last ten days," I say, careful to avoid specificity, in case she's trying to sucker me into giving her information she doesn't in fact have. To push the point, I add, "Where was I, and how did you know?"

"You were hospitalized due to an incident

that took place here," she says. "Involving guns and a helicopter, I believe."

"And?"

"And how do I know? Hmm. A reporter does not reveal her sources. That may upset you right now, but should you and I share other *interesting* information, you'll be the beneficiary of the same type of confidentiality."

"Surely you don't expect me to spill precious beans in front of a camera."

"Of course not," she says. "Today we deal with more immediate things."

"My image, my brand."

She shrugs. "Whatever you want to call it. We discuss the two things we worked out with your agent."

I pull out my phone and review the two line items in my agent's latest text: why I've been MIA from the task force for ten days, now going on eleven, and the Purple Heart thing.

"OK," I say.

"You want to go through some sample questions and answers, just to warm up?"

"Nah."

She smiles, and I don't know if it's because she approves or because it works to her advantage.

"What's in it for you?" I ask her. "Me, doing this fluff piece with you."

"First of all, when you and I are done, this will be anything but fluffy. Second, I'm not here to do you a favor. This is a good, solid story for which I have the exclusive, per our agreement." She points back toward the house, and I presume the gate into my property. "They lose, I win. That's plenty in it for me."

"But this is not all you want."

"I want to earn your trust. That's thing three, yes. And I want to earn your trust so that you and I can discuss more important things, if and when you're up to it."

"And what would these important things be?"

"You sure you want to get into that now?"

"Maybe not all the way, but enough for me to get a preview of coming attractions."

Bridget smiles at that. "I love how you phrase things. It's part of why people love you,

you know."

I stare back at her, unflinching until her smile falls off her lips.

"Very well," she says. "Someday, I'd like to talk about your recovery, your special, military-issue prosthetic legs, and any other gadgets that may have gone into you to bring about what everyone rightfully considers a most remarkable bounce-back."

"Into me? What the hell are you talking about?" I ask, thinking of the one thing I know went into Shadow.

She stops to gauge me. "You don't know."

"Know what?"

We hear steps coming up the path, and she leans in. "Let's take care of thing one and thing two right now. We'll talk about the rest when you're ready."

Her camera man and his assistant arrive carting all sorts of things, up to and including two director chairs. His vision for the interview has us sitting in front of the barn. She tells him, nonsense, we have to be walking and standing. Does she have to think of everything? They go back and forth on that for the short minute it takes her to assert her will and vision on the situation. I get to thinking I like her a little more for that, how she knows what she wants, takes control, and leads with it.

We shoot the first segment with me and her walking slowly from the path and up to the barn. Her camera man walks backward in front of us with one camera, with another camera shooting a wide angle from a tripod while the assistant stays out of shot holding a large reflector to shield us from the harshest of the pre-noon sunlight.

Bridget launches off with a comment about realizing we can't discuss much about the investigation given its sensitivity.

I respond with, "While I cannot say much, like you say, I can tell you we have a great team working this, best minds in law enforcement. I have confidence they'll get to the bottom of this."

"You say *they...* Some people have noted you're not taking an active part in the investigation."

"Well, to be frank, out of all those sharp people on the task force, I'm not the one that's going to get the jar lid open. Not by a long shot. Truth is what I can do to help is very limited. I got some great dogs, but they don't have any intelligence on where those creeps might strike next, where they're hiding now, and none of that other stuff." I tap my nose. "They just have some great sniffers, but unless they're on top of the explosive material, they ain't gonna solve this."

She smiles for me and for the camera. "But still, with what happened this morning, people are wondering why you're not more involved."

"I'm terribly sorry about what happened in Miami this morning. Horrible thing for all the families and loved ones involved. There wasn't anything I could do about it, as much as I wish there was."

"What can you tell us about where you've been the last ten days?" she asks, and now I'm thinking this is it. We're into it.

We've reached the barn and stand there. Before I can answer, she turns and makes a neck-cutting sign.

"Alright," she says turning back to me. She takes me by the shoulders and turns me to my right. "There, that's better light vs. pose." She's looking up at me. "OK, so now you know what the question is and you won't be surprised."

"Did I look that stunned?"

"A little. You know what you want to say?"

"Yeah, maybe."

"No maybe about it. Just the answer: lock, load, aim, fire." She shrugs. "OK, so I'm not so good with military illustrations, but you get the point."

"I do."

"No hesitation."

"None."

"Because hesitation breeds and communicates doubt."

"Got it," I say, getting a little tired of the impromptu tutorial, while at the same time I wonder why she's going out of her way to make me look good.

"Super." Without turning, she takes a step back and smiles at me. "Rolling?"

"Rolling."

With a near exact replica of her intonation when she first asked it, she restarts. "What can you tell us about where you've been the last ten days?"

"Again, to be truthful, I can't put out the hours the other folks on the task force put out."

"Why's that?"

"The fact that I came back with less than two legs is bad enough. Tough enough on the body and the mind." I pause, and she lets me run the clock, nodding at me with tightened lips. "I came back damaged in more ways, if you know what I mean."

"PTSD."

"That's an acronym. It doesn't have H in it, so I reckon it's not the right one. H for hell, I mean. The hell we've seen. The hell we bring back with us. The hell inside our heads that keeps firing up every time we think life's gonna cut us a break, finally, and then it burns again."

"You're hurting, still."

"Yeah. People may look at me, see me on TV hiking down some mountain trail or walking into a building with my dogs, and they'll have no idea. Not a clue what happens in your soul when you see a bombed out terminal with bodies mangled and all torn up. Not the faintest imagining of what it's like to smell the residue of explosives and the scent of burned flesh and overheated blood."

"It puts you back in the war zone."

"That, and you realize the war zone followed you home. It's here, not just in your head, but all around you. You thought you were fighting on some distant land to keep the war there, to make it stop, if that was possible. But no. It's here."

"Seeing that affected you deeply," she says, and I realize she's sounding like my therapist, making short little statements to keep me on the line and talking.

"Sure. So, I needed some time off."

"To take care of yourself."

I look her in the eye as I'm about to rip away from her one thing she thinks she's holding over me. "To let kind people take care of me. Meaning, I was in a hospital." I smile at her now. "Enough said on that topic, I guess."

She nods, then makes that cutting-neck motion again. "Good," she says to no one in particular as she fusses with her hair, which a stiff breeze from the Rockies has twirled around some.

"Well, that should shut up the missing-for-ten-days crowd," the camera man notes with a smile.

"Yes, I should say so," Bridget replies, now looking up at me again with her smile. "Right down the middle, no fancy stuff. Well played."

"I don't play," I reply with as blank an expression as I can paint on my face.

"No, I suppose you don't have much use for games, do you? You just do, which is why I think I'm going to really love you."

"I don't play on the all-girls team, neither."

"Ooh, that we'll definitely expunge from the record." She winks at me. "OK, so how about we walk from the other direction and let's see if we can do as well on thing two as we did on thing one."

A narrower trail curls through the ranch

until it disappears at a thick cluster of aspens toward the southern fence. We walk up that trail and turn around to make our way back.

"Rolling," the camera man says.

"You've been wounded twice, during two separate tours," Bridget says, the question hidden in there somewhere.

"Yes. During my last two tours, both times in Afghanistan."

"And you received a Purple Heart the first time?"

"Yes. I just had it mailed to me, though. I didn't want the ceremony."

"Why? Why not be honored?"

"It was barely a scratch. OK, so I have a bullet hole above my right hip. Truth is that night many of my buddies died."

"But the ones that lived while you manned a machine gun, they lived because of you."

"Yeah, maybe. Whatever the case, it didn't feel right. No disrespect to other veterans, but for me, I just wanted to move on."

"But then, when you returned from your last deployment, now a double amputee, you returned it. Not only that, but you wouldn't accept the second medal that your injuries earned you. Why? Were you angry?"

"I was many things. Drugged up from the pain killers. Depressed. Bitter. Yeah, I guess I was angry."

"That must have been a very deep anger."

"It was. As it should be. I know some people think I'm angry at my country. That don't make no sense. I still live here, I still serve here, in the Reserves, so there goes that theory. Some might say I was angry at the President, who's even offered to pin on those medals himself. But I voted for him, twice, second time just last fall, so there goes that, too."

"Were you angry at the military, at war in general?"

"War, yeah. Always be angry at it, hate it. The military, I guess there's some of that. But most of all, I'm angry at what happened to me that night when that IED cut me up. That includes what happened minutes before the IED went off."

I see her mouth moving, but I don't hear her

question. A breeze kicks up and rustles through the nearby aspens. I do hear it. It's all I hear during the moment when I know what I must say next.

"I was raped," I say. "Gang-raped."

I see her mouth open, but no words come out.

"That night two things were taken from me: my virginity and my legs. So when people go on and on about things you pin on your chest, I do some head-scratching. Maybe it's because they don't know. Now they do. Purple hearts are one thing, but if I may be crude here for a second, I wish somebody could give me back my red cherry."

Bridget covers her mouth and nose, her eyes large above her hand before she turns to her camera man to give him the neck cut sign. She's stays like that, with her back half-turned to me.

"I take it you got what you needed?" I ask her. My voice comes out raspy, a shade short of a growl.

She doesn't answer. Behind her, the camera man is setting the camera down so he can rub his neck. The assistant lowers the reflector so that in front of him it looks like an overgrown apron.

"You weren't raped by Afghanis, were you?" Bridget asks finally.

"Not so much."

Bridget manages to gather herself enough to ask whether I want to talk more about the rape, who did it, why it wasn't reported, and so on. I say that I don't see the point and suggest we head back to get the cover shots of me interacting with my dogs, maybe running them through one of their training drills. After some fruitless back and forth, we start off trail to meet up with the dogs.

Once all the dog and doggy show comes to an end, Bridget and her crew walk back up the road toward the gate, and I go in the house. I radio Cassandra to stay put by the gate while I eye Allison fussing around the kitchen. It takes a second for my brain to register why the kitchen lies in such upheaval. Allison has gone master baker on me.

"That's a heck of a lot of brownies and cookies. Who's gonna eat all those?"

"Guess."

"You did all that while we were out there?"

"You guys have been at it for three hours. I had plenty of time to come up with great ideas."

I eye the clock and realize I've lost all track of time. "Noon," I mutter. "So those dear folks out there are going to be having their lunches, and we're going to provide them with some dessert."

"You're catching on."

"How… thoughtful of me," I say.

"You don't sound appreciative."

"That's just me being my usual non-charming self. It's actually a good idea."

"You serious?" Allison asks.

"What? You didn't think so? You just made them expecting me to chew you out for it?"

"Let's say I expected a little resistance, with my kind heart and persuasive ways winning the day in the end."

I curl my lips and shake my head, resisting the urge to grin. "Fine. I'll help you take them out."

"You sure? I thought I'd take them out myself."

"And what's the point in that? To make you real popular? No, we need a different message, a brand polishing, as it were. The big mean dog trainer, killer girl takes cookies out to the reporters."

"Guess you have a point." Allison grins at me, making me think I've walked into the very idea she had all along.

She uses a couple of aluminum foil covered flat baking sheets, stacking the brownies on one, the cookies on the other, each layer in the stack separated by more aluminum foil. She takes one of the makeshift platters, and I carry the other. Out of the house, through the yard and down the road we go.

Halfway there, Cassandra turns to cast a look of disbelief and disapproval in our direction. Shady runs back to meet us, with

Rover not far behind. When we get to the gate, the reporters start shouting questions. I smile, say hello, tell them we have some goodies for them. I even make a point to make eye contact with each of the video cameras pointed in my direction.

We let Allison take care of the hospitality on the other side of the fence. At one point I lean in to Cassandra to whisper in her ear, "It's OK, I'll keep my mouth shut."

With that, I drape my arms over the gate, and smile as I watch Allison play hostess. At one point I relax enough to rest my chin on my forearm. Out of the corner of my eye I see a photographer snap a few shots of me for the few moments I allow myself to remain in that pose.

An hour later, while browsing the Internet back in the house, we'll see a photo showing me smiling, arms on the fence, chin on my forearm, soft cloud-diffused light coloring my cheeks, and shimmering aspens with leaves turning yellow in a soft-focus background. That photo will go viral. My agent will call me, and for once I will answer her call so she can tell me "that was just fab-genius."

And that's before my interview with Bridget hits the air later that evening. After dinner, I sit out on the porch while Cassandra and Allison keep watching TV and checking the Internet for more Jane McMurtry sightings. It appears my image has undergone full rehabilitation, easy peasy.

Now I have to figure out what else I'm going to do with that.

Later that night, as I prepare to go to bed, I get a text from Dan.

"Beautiful photo," it says. "Now my phone's backdrop."

Whatever comes next, I have no choice but to smile at that.

Chapter 12

Aiming for a semi-long speed run the next morning, we keep our dinner to a carbo-load, non-alcoholic affair. First thing in the morning, Allison drives back to her place and returns dressed in a fresh, new looking running outfit, and carrying a bag of clothes and personal items. I've told her I'd like her to start moving in before we get the barn fixed up, and she's not about to postpone taking me up on the offer.

Before my hospital stay, Cassandra traced a six mile route along my property. Six-point-two miles, to be precise, since she wanted to achieve a 10K course. Just after 7:30 AM we start running it at an easy warmup place. Cassandra has warned us: at the one mile marker we're going to push it as hard as I can run it, seeing as to how I'm the limiting reagent in this operation. Well, Allison, who's still sore from the thirteen miler two days prior, will probably not super-perform today either.

As for Shady and Shadow, especially Shadow, they seem to be feeling no ill effects from the Sunday long run. Dogs tend to mask their pain well, though, and I'm wondering in particular how all this is affecting their joints. Even Shadow's special hip gadget.

"So how does this work again?" Allison asks, her voice registering apprehension.

Cassandra answers with, "Warm up for a mile, go hard for one mile, easy for a half, hard for one mile, easy for half, hard one more mile, easy on the last half plus change up the finish like."

"Don't do math in public," I tell Allison with a grin.

"No kidding."

"You always do the math up front," Cassandra says. "One, plus three times one, plus three times a half equals five and a half, plus the cool-down point-seven miles at the end, brings us to six point-two miles."

"Right," Allison says, like someone who's not concerned so much about the numbers as she is about what they represent.

As we run, we keep the dogs on leash, same way they'll trot with us on the marathon. Last night we discussed whether we should run them more than the previously planned ten miles at the end of the race. We consider that since they did so well during the thirteen miler. Cassandra wants to wait to make the decision. I don't. Ten is plenty by my account.

"We'll see how the dogs do after today," I say now. "If they start feeling ill effects from over-training, this might be a good spot check."

"They're doing fine," Cassandra says. "They're eating it up. Look at them."

"Still, I think Jane's right," Allison puts in. "We should keep an eye on them."

"Sure. There's no harm in that," Cassandra says, checking her watch and ready to refocus on the task at hand.

This little conversation gives me an idea. My mind makes a connection between keeping an eye on the dog's health, whatever's ticking in Shadow's hip, and what Bridget said to me yesterday. *Gadgets that may have gone into you…*

"How's your schedule looking the rest of the day?" I ask Allison.

"A couple of appointments in the morning, one procedure in the afternoon, 2 PM. Should be done by three. Why?"

I make sure that Cassandra, who's leading the way can't see it before I shoot Allison a raised eyebrow. "Maybe I can bring Shadow in, have you do one of your tests. Shady, too, like you did for her a while back. Joints and such. Make sure all this running isn't tearing them up."

I say this hoping with her body language Cassandra shows us whether she's with us or against us.

"Cassandra can stay at the house," I add. "In case more reporters come calling and need to be set in their place."

"OK," Allison says. "Come by three, but it may be more like three thirty if the procedure runs long."

"Sure."

I wink at her and turn to face straight ahead. Cassandra's body language remains strictly that of a runner at work.

By my GPS watch, we're nearing the one mile mark. Now the fun will start. As I get ready to press, I think of how no one ever asked about the disc. Not Cassandra, not Allison, not anyone at the hospital, though there my recollection may have succumbed to a steady medication drip.

I know they never found it, because they couldn't have found it. Not without digging up half the ranch to figure out where I buried it.

Allison doesn't make it past the first three miles. Cassandra, the dogs and I finish out the workout while Allison limps back toward the house. We find her on the porch, sitting on the deck with her back against one of the wood columns, her strained ankle resting on an ice bag.

"The ice will help," Cassandra says.

I'm having my doubts. An iffy Achilles tendon takes a lot of time to heal, and with a little over three weeks before the marathon, I'm thinking this injury is pretty much terminal. I feared this much for Allison. Training for a marathon is brutal enough if you can start months ahead, but short-cutting it to a couple of months like she's trying to do often spells disaster unless you're already in shape to run long distances. In retrospect, I'm kicking myself a little for allowing her to do the speed run, as that is one of the ways to overstress and injure yourself.

"How fast did you guys end up going?" Allison asks.

Cassandra is already checking the stats on her GPS watch. "Fastest pace was the second interval. Eight-oh-two pace." She looks up at me with a grin.

I shake my head. "That explains why I was feeling like someone was pulling me by the neck with a rope tied to a galloping horse."

"Jane, that's awesome!" Allison says.

"You've always said how you're not a fast runner. It's looking like your Clydesdale days are over!"

I don't quite know how to respond to that, since the Clydesdale reference harks back to my own self-deprecation. I also don't want to admit—to them or to myself, I can't decide— that I've never run a mile faster than nine minute pace. Ever. Not even in high school when I was part of the track team as a shot putter. And I'm heavier now, minus two half legs, of course.

"Well, I sure ain't going to run the marathon at that pace," I say.

"That's not the point of the speed runs," Cassandra says. "If you do it right, they do make you a little faster during marathon day, but not at that pace. For you, I'm thinking maybe a little north of ten minute pace might work."

I shrug, and we make some additional inconsequential banter before we head inside the house for breakfast. Cassandra goes in first, offering to cook us some *huevos rancheros*. I stay behind to help Allison to her feet, resisting the urge to wince when I see how heavily she's limping.

"I really screwed myself over, huh, Jane?"

We walk together to the front door, and I open it up for her. "I have some sport's tape. We'll wrap up the ankle before you go. Fortunately it's your left, so it shouldn't affect your driving, especially with an automatic."

"OK," she grunts more than says.

I lower my voice. "Listen, Allison. This afternoon, that check I want you to do."

"Yeah?"

"It's not for the dogs." I watch her face crease into a frown. In reply to the implied question I tap on my chest.

I arrive at the hospital with Shady and Shadow a little before 3 PM. The place strikes me as so familiar. And yet, memories of the last time I came here to have Allison run an MRI on Shadow seem so distant now.

Allison meets us in the hallway. She walks us into the lab saying we have a small window before the next appointment comes in for an MRI. This time she takes us to a different room where a bigger machine resides. The one they use for larger animals.

"I don't know whether to be offended at that," I say.

"Well, as they'd say at church, God's blessed you with a bounty." She says that mimicking my preacher's accent.

"For someone that don't warm a pew often, you sure retain a lot," I jibe back at her.

"It's how I made it through school. I slept in for all my morning classes, but managed to grab enough on the occasional day when I wasn't hung over from the latest dorm party."

"You might want to quit right there. I don't think the doctor-patient privilege works the opposite way."

Allison waves off my comment and starts setting up the machine. She's working fast, and if I'm not mistaken, her hands are shaking a bit. From her purse she takes out a small hard drive. She holds it out for a second in her quivering hand, as if I need to inspect and approve it.

"I figured out how to record to an external drive without leaving a trace in the system," she whispers. Her lips close tight, and she looks up at me.

"Good idea," I say, somewhat ashamed I haven't really worked this out for myself, and that I'm putting her out like this. "Thank you," I add, as if that makes it better.

She turns her back to me and starts plugging stuff and click-clacking on the keyboard. "You never told me about the disc."

"They don't have it."

"Good." She points me at the slot where I'll have to wedge myself and lie down. "You don't have to disrobe all the way. Just take off anything metal."

It doesn't take me long to comply, including the removal of my legs. She helps me get in there and shows me how to lie down. Over the next ten minutes we take four sets of scans. One with me lying on my back, one on my right side, another on my stomach, and the final one on my left side.

She helps me out, and while I re-attach everything I took off, she works at the computer, telling me she's removing the temporary system files.

We walk out at the same time another team is coming in to prep for their non-human patient's scan.

"Alright," she says handing me the drive in the hallway. "That's got everything. Wrap it up real good if it's going outdoors, and bury it wherever you want."

I take it and go to leave, but she grabs me by the forearm.

"Before you stash it, let's take a look at it in my laptop, OK?" Allison says.

"Tonight?" I say.

She looks over her shoulder then back at me. "Yeah. Let's plan on that."

Chapter 13

I arrive at the barn first. By the time Allison and her boyfriend get there five minutes later, I have already concealed the hard drive. Allison's boyfriend comes into the barn carrying a cardboard box of her camping gear. An air mattress and sleeping bag, she explains, which she will use tonight when she spends the first night here.

"It's going to be cold here," I object. "I thought you weren't moving in here until we have it reconfigured." I'm trying not to be annoyed from the appearance that she's trying to lay the squatter's claim since, after all, I haven't yet fully agreed to this arrangement.

"It will let us know how much insulation we need," Allison explains.

I dismiss that with a shrug. "You ain't gonna have the slightest idea how much insulation it takes until winter hits."

Her boyfriend stands, holding the box, his gaze ping-ponging between her and me. I take the measure of him quick enough, a lean, muscular and more tanned than I expected man. By tanned I'm meaning I think he's of mixed heritage, probably a little of African, maybe some Indian—not sure about that last part.

He notices me looking at him. With that he tucks the box under his left arm and extends his right hand. "My name is Esteban Ibarra," he says.

His handshake is firm and warm.

"Nice to meet you," I say. "I guess both Allison and I forgot our manners."

"Mind if I look around and start measuring while you two talk?"

"Sure," I reply, thinking to myself he's pretty sharp for wanting to get away from our bickering.

Before I have much more time to reflect on

that, he's set Allison's box down and is walking
back to Allison's car to grab his tools. He comes
back wearing his tool belt, and we head inside,
Allison's and my spat forgotten.

The barn stands as the tallest and newest
structure in the property, something Dad built
after he bought the ranch. Nonetheless, through
disuse and lack of upkeep over the course of
more than a decade, it's fallen into disrepair.
Upon entering we start walking down a wide
corridor lined with stalls and crumbling bales
of hay.

"These are the ones I told you we might
retrofit for smaller animals," Allison says to
Esteban, pointing to the narrower stalls on the
left. In contrast to the right side stalls, sized for
horses, Dad intended the left bank of stalls for
housing animals in the winter, but they still
exceed the size one would need for sick or
boarded pets of the sort Allison has in mind.

"I thought we're measuring the loft today,"
Esteban says with the tone of a person who
likes to stay focused on a single task and carry
it out without distractions.

"We are," Allison replies. "I just wanted to point it out, you know, so you can start conceptualizing."

He shrugs at that and looks at me. I point him down toward the far end of the barn, and we resume our walk.

The loft amounts to little more than a platform built about twelve feet off the ground, toward the back of the barn. Given the depth of the barn, it takes another thirty seconds to arrive at the point where we can stare up at the loft and the ladder leading up to it. From where we stand, we can see some of the sparse furniture up there, as well as the window that looks out to an aspen grove not far from the back of the barn.

Esteban pats a rung of the ladder. "Probably want stairs, yes?"

"Is there room?" Allison asks.

With a puzzled frown, he looks around, then at her. I like him a little more when he doesn't say it, as the obvious answer lies all around us. Room does not appear in short supply here.

"We make it an up and turn ninety degrees to save space, yes?" he says. "It'll look better, too," he adds looking at me.

Esteban climbs up the ladder and starts looking around. After making a few measurements and taking some notes he comes down. Over the next few minutes, he throws out a few ideas, some expensive, like installing a large window that looks down to the barn floor and stalls, and when I frown at the sound of ringing cash registers, he offers more sensible options, like a smaller window. We talk about adding walls, how to insulate them, what kind of sensible flooring to install, and so on. Finally, he brings up cabinetry, and I say we'll think about it, again, fearing the expanding price tag I'll get. I ask him a few more questions about electrical and such. He says he'll look into it, include it in his bid, and we're done.

His truck stayed back at the house, at my request, so we shake hands, and off he goes with his tools. Just as he's about to leave, I shout after him to ask if he's got dinner plans. He says, no, not really, and when I offer he join us, he accepts. I note a skip in his step as he leaves us.

"Nice guy," I tell Allison. "Like the accent."

"He's a hard worker."

"I bet." I wink at her, and we start laughing.

"Anyway," I say when we settle down. "You got your laptop handy?"

She returns a minute later with her laptop. I show her where I stashed the hard drive, behind a lose board in horse stall number 5, and she agrees this is where we'll keep it from now on.

"There's a desk up there," I say, pointing up at the loft.

She goes up the ladder first, her laptop case slung over her neck and at her back. I follow her. Only when I reach the top do I ask myself: have I ever climbed a ladder with my new legs? I can't say that I have. And yet here I am standing on this deck, twelve feet above ground, wondering whether what Allison is about to show me will explain my fireman-like agility.

"So much room up here," Allison is saying

while she waits for her computer to boot up.

I look around and guess she's right, though I haven't been much up here since Dad died. This was his office when he came here. A beat-up metal desk and swiveling, creaky chair align against the window. He loved sitting there and looking out to the aspens, especially in the fall, when he and I would come down here from Wyoming, my Mom and brother wanting no part of our excursion. I remember standing here with Dad, looking over his shoulder at the trees, their leaves turning gold like they are now. I zone out a tad as I stare at them now. For a few moments, my eyes decipher a shape, a dog's head drawn by the highlights and shadows in the foliage. Rover's head.

"You OK?" Allison asks.

"Yeah," I say, wiping at my eyes. "What you got?"

"Hold on, let me connect the hard drive."

It takes her another minute or so to register the drive on her computer, and a couple more to access it with the MRI viewer software. She brings up the view of me lying on my back first.

It stops her short right away.

"Do you see it?" she asks.

"I'm not sure."

She replays the slices and taps the screen at three places, my hips, and what looks like my spine, as seen from the front.

"Here," she says. "Let's try the one hundred and eighty degree offset to make sure." In short order she brings up the view of my lying on my stomach. The spots show clearer now, brighter, especially the one at the small of my back. Together they form a triangle.

Allison zooms in to the spot at the bottom of my spine and replays the slices.

"Gears," I say.

"A mechanism of some sort. Very small."

I pull another chair and sit. "Just like Shadow's."

By way of response, Allison accesses a view were I'm lying on my side. She zooms in again, and taps on the screen. She doesn't need to say it. Though I could go and dig up the CD to compare, I don't have to. Whatever the nature and purpose of that gadget, it resembles

Shadow's. Same design, maybe a different dash model number, I'm guessing.

Allison's already finding the final view, the one of me lying on my other side. We see the mirror image of what we saw a second ago.

"Have you ever gotten your medical records?" Allison asks. "All of them?"

I sigh. I've never even thought to ask for them.

"It might be a good time to ask," she says.

"What are you thinking?"

"Well, your records won't contain a full accounting of these things they put in you. I'm pretty sure of that, hush-hush national security and all. But they might contain a full accounting of your injuries."

"Might?"

"If they didn't cover it up."

"Cover up what?"

"This is conjecture on my part," she says. "I can only guess."

I stare out to the aspens. Their golden splendor dims in the waning sunlight. Rover's head has disappeared.

"Permission to guess granted," I tell her.

"I'm guessing you sustained spinal and perhaps even hip injuries. I'm guessing those gadgets helped you get back on your feet." She pauses, and in the silence I have but to guess at what she says next.

"Remember that time we looked into the company that makes your prosthetics?"

"Energetix."

"Remember the gyro technology they tried to license?"

"Yeah."

"It doesn't work except as part of a system, remember that?"

"Mmm-hmm."

"I'm guessing your prosthetic legs work in sync with these gadgets. Wirelessly perhaps. To make a full system. To balance you."

I recall again how we looked into Energetix. Now I'm seeing the connection we missed then. Why they were so interested in me. It wasn't all about my legs.

"You're thinking Energetix did this." I say.

"Hard to tell. It's blue sky stuff, people

dreaming of what could be. A machine's one thing, but making this work inside a person's body... Anyway, you'd think there'd be patents out there if people figured this out."

I nod, but inside I'm thinking, *not if it's classified*.

Allison adds, "But yes. I've heard of theories about how to reverse nerve damage with electrical devices that interact with your neural network. All theory." She bites her lip. "Or maybe someone's figured it out."

"So what you're saying is I'm a walking science experiment. Without my knowing."

"Yeah."

I hear her tapping on her keyboard, perhaps to bring back another view and take a closer look. I don't care anymore. My gaze stays on the aspens, watching the last of their color give way to shadow and darkness.

The walkie talkie at my belt squawks. I answer it, and Cassandra says, "We got visitors."

"Who?" I ask.

"Brady's crew. At the main gate, asking for

permission to come in. Want to talk with you. Say the word, and I tell them to scatter."

"Brady there?"

"Yeah, but they say he doesn't have to come in if you don't want to see him."

I take that in for a moment. My guess is that Cassandra already told Brady he best stay away. Don't want to unravel me again. And if she knows what I know now or has an inkling of it, I'm sure she's impressed it upon them that they best not rattle me too much, seeing as to how much they got riding in me.

"Who else is there?" I ask.

"Two doctors. That shrink you've been seeing at the base, and a surgeon. Says he's the one that operated on you."

"Guess he wants to catch up."

"My guess, too," Cassandra replies.

"OK, let me get to the house, and you and I will talk about it."

"I'll tell them to stand by."

I stand up and clip the radio back on my belt.

"You think they know?" Allison asks.

"I don't think it much matters."

She unplugs and hands me the portable drive. I climb down the ladder, now with full appreciation for what makes my agility and dexterity possible. After I hide the drive in stall number five, Allison and I drive back to the house.

"I think we best tell Esteban that we'll give him a rain check on dinner," I say.

Allison doesn't disagree.

Chapter 14

It's hard, and I do it with gritted teeth, but I cook dinner, then let them come in. All of them. Let's break bread together, reason together, maybe bend a couple of swords into plowshares and toss up a few doves into the air while we're at it. I don't know why I do it this way either, but when Cassandra questions my gracious hospitable spirit, I quote her a Bible verse.

"If your enemy is hungry, feed him; if he is thirsty, give him something to drink. In doing this, you will heap burning coals on his head."

"Romans twelve twenty," Cassandra says without hesitation.

"If you say so," I reply with a grin. "Keep in mind I'm focusing primarily on the burning coals on their heads part."

She grins back. "You sure?"

I slap my hips. "Why wouldn't I be?"

She frowns like she doesn't understand my gesture.

"Never mind," I say, wondering now how much she really knows. Maybe they told her about the magic legs, maybe they went as far as to divulge Shadow's gadgetry, but not everything. After all, the best way to conceal truth is under other truth.

While I cook, Allison and Cassandra set the dining room table. They stretch it out and jam an extra leaf in it, and they get out my mother's china.

Our guests come rolling in a little after 7 PM: Lieutenant Colonel Brady, doctors Taylor and Sven, along with a Major Someone who's coming along for the experience and will keep his mouth shut all evening long, even if the way he keeps looking at me gives off a bad vibe. We agree to leave business for after dinner, and so we make cordial chit-chat over breaded chicken, mashed potatoes, broccoli and a simple lettuce with cucumbers and tomatoes salad.

As I serve the dessert and coffee, I give the go ahead for their in-brief to commence.

"Should she be here for that?" Cassandra asks, pointing at Allison.

"Yes, she should," I say. I stare Brady down and ask him, "Any reason she should go?"

"She can stay."

"Thought so."

Now Allison is looking at me, puzzled.

"Yeah, girl," I tell her. "They know you know. And before you ask how that may be the case, what do you think they did to this place while I was convalescing at that hospital?" I turn to Brady. "I bet some of your best bugs went right to that loft in that there barn down yonder. Nothing escapes your scrutiny, huh, Brady?"

Allison opens her mouth and finally lands on her question. "Then why did you agree to talk in there?"

"Because I ain't pining for the clandestine life. Last thing I wanna do is go hiding behind trees so as I can have my privacy. They wanna poke into my life, go ahead. Out in the open, as my momma used to say, in the full of sunlight, that's where oozing wounds don't fester."

Allison opens her mouth again, but this time there ain't no reason for anything to come out, so it doesn't. For her part, Cassandra's face shows she's the least in-the-know of us all, and I feel for her.

"I reckon there ain't much you can tell me I don't already know or can't make an educated guess on." I tilt my head toward Cassandra. "But for the sake of some of us, how's about you go ahead and say your peace. Might help cleanse your soul a bit, even if it don't have the same effect on our palate."

Doctor Sven, my surgeon and alleged savior trades a look with Taylor, the one who's so far failed to score similar success with my mind— or my soul, as the case may be. She gives him a tight little nod, and he plows through his dissertation. What he tells us more or less confirms Allison's guesses back at the barn.

When he's done, Brady says, "I know we did this without your consent, but hell if I was going to let you come back paralyzed, girl."

"The human mind excels at convenient rationalization, and hitched to a dark soul, it twists truth beyond recognition." I stare at Brady. "Know who said that?"

He shrugs. "I'm not as educated as you."

"I did," I say. "Just now. Thanks for the inspiration."

"Major," Sven says leaning forward over the table, as if imploring my mercy. "Part of the reason we didn't tell you is because we didn't think you were ready to accept so much all at once. We were planning to tell you all along, once we felt you were—"

"Stable," I say to complete his sentence. "Probably a cool call. I was so doped up on pain killers I doubt I would've grasped a single word you said about this technical marvel of yours."

"We also wanted to keep the program secret, under wraps until—"

"Until people can get over their RoboCop phobias," I say, all too glad to cut him off again.

"Until the technology is ready," Sven says

evenly.

"So you plugged it in me without knowing it's ready. That's awful sweet of you. Do tell me where to send the thank you card."

"Think of how many wounded soldiers will benefit from this," Sven says. "There used to be a time when soldiers with your type of injuries wouldn't make it past the field hospital. But now, with the advances we've made in medicine, we can save so many more lives—"

"But you can't restore them," Cassandra says with a cool edge to her voice. "You can bring them back alive, but you can't give them good lives. Now you think you have a way out."

"Yes, they do," I say. "A way for politicians to not feel so bad about sending us into the grinder. A way to not have to keep staring at us, or worse, pretending we're not there in towns, vet hospitals, and wherever else we dare show our sorry bodies."

Sven sits back in his chair, folds his hands on his lap, and looks down at his empty dessert plate. I look there, too, tracing the golden, weaving pattern along the plate's rim. I remember momma now, giving me those plates before we took her to the convalescent home, holding one just like it in her hands, touching the pattern with her curled, arthritic fingers.

"You may not feel like it right now, Jane," Taylor says. "But you've been given a great gift. And with it a responsibility."

I look up at her. "You kidding, right? You're not dropping the GI Jane, comic book rah-rah speech on me, are you?"

"Think of what you represent," Taylor replies. "Hope for so many. Already people are looking up to you. They are finding inspiration in your struggle and how you overcome it. How you are overcoming it every day."

"Right," Allison says. "So she's your poster girl now."

"That's a very shallow way of putting it."

"You know people are already speculating about her," Allison says. "They're already guessing that there's no way someone could do what she's doing."

"We wanted to discuss that," Brady replies.

"We want to coordinate a statement with you about how your prosthetic legs are part of a military sponsored test trial you are taking part in."

"But nothing else," I say.

Brady nods. "That's correct."

I don't say it, but there it is again. The best way to conceal truth is under other truth. I think back to Energetix, and its owner, Devon Smith, and imagine how this announcement will give his stock price a nice bump. Part of me don't want to play no part in that, but the other part, the one that wants to get on with life wins out.

"Alright," I say getting up from the table. "I think we've beaten that horse well enough."

Sven, Taylor, Brady and their Major Something-or-other exchange looks. That's it? they seem to be asking one another. Didn't we come here ready for more?

"So you're on board," Brady says.

"Not unless he asks and says pretty please," I shoot back.

"Who?"

"Who else? The Commander in Chief. I hope he's briefed on this. Heck, I bet he came up with the whole idea himself, and if he didn't, he'll say so in his next speech, anyway."

The call comes an hour later. Truth is I'm not ready for it. I thought at the earliest it would happen the following day on account of the time zone difference. But they call my bluff, and when that happens, you can do nothing else but to turn them cards. So there I am in my kitchen, everyone looking at me while I clench my landline phone receiver against my ear, and I got some crappy cards to turn over.

"Yes, Mr. President, I understand your request," I say. "I hope you're right and that this does a lot of good for soldiers and civilians alike, like you envision."

I pause there. I've heard nobody says no the President. When he calls on you to serve your country, you just say yes, no matter what manner of sacrifice you have to make or how much you'd rather be doing something else. For a brief moment, I entertain whether I should join the few that dare go against that tide. But I don't have the heart for it. And at that moment, I'm glad I don't.

"You will have my cooperation, Mr. President."

"And your decorations."

"I'll be glad to come to your house to receive them," I say.

"Sounds like a plan, then," he says. "And it's your house, too, by the way." He thanks me, and we hang up.

I glance over at the stove clock to note no more than three minutes have passed, and that includes me waiting on hold while the leader of the free world came on the line. Guess that tells me how much I really wanted to push back on this, my newest mission.

The rest is details for Brady to outline: what comes next; how Allison will have to sign confidentiality agreements safeguarding the project; the turning over of all files she and I generated from scans of Shadow's and my body; how we'll deal with the media, especially one Bridget Suarez; and how we'll use the upcoming Marine Corps Marathon to make the announcement about my wondrous prosthetic legs. Somewhere in there, the President himself will present me with two Purple hearts at the White House. Everyone's thinking Monday after the marathon will suit best.

"And then there's one more matter," I say to Brady.

"Yes."

"I take it he's around the corner."

"On call, five minutes away," Brady replies.

"Alright, then," I say. "Tell Special Agent Dan Murphy we'll brew a fresh pot of coffee for him, and we still got some desert for him if he'll have it."

Chapter 15

"How long have you known about this?" I ask Dan from one of my living room reclining chairs.

"Which part?" Dan asks.

My gaze drifts and meanders along the tapestry pattern of yellowing drapes I've told myself I should replace. With Sven and the major gone back to the car, Brady and Taylor are sitting on the sofa, sinking into it is more like it, while Dan makes his pitch from a love seat next to my chair.

I say, "Yeah, sorry. With so many parts, guess I should've been more specific."

"We knew it wasn't just Iraqi nationals when Miami happened."

"Right, two farm-raised dog handlers there.

One from Iowa, the other from Nebraska. Don't get more apple pie than that."

"Right."

"And that leads you to think this is some group of disgruntled vets, maybe a little PTSD-cooked."

"Something along those lines."

"They got a hold of a few Iraqi buddies now stateside, and they have the connections back there to blackmail them with their families."

"You got it."

"Wanna bring the war home, let us all appreciate the horrors." I'm paraphrasing now, recapping what he said over the past twenty minutes in my own abridged version. I hate to repeat things, but I'm leading up to my point.

"Yeah," Dan replies.

"Kind'a like those three guys stuffing kids hooked up to IEDs under rock piles." I eye Brady. "Which is why the Colonel is paying such close attention."

Brady shifts in his seat and raises his chin a bit.

"Possibly," Dan says.

"Birds of the same feather from where I'm sitting," I say.

"We're looking into it."

"You best do that. I bet you're also looking into how all this wraps around all the way back to me. Like for instance, what can I do to help you solve this case other than sniff around for bombs?"

Dan swallows, looks down at his hands for a bit, then raises his gaze and looks across at Brady. "We got a note. From the bombers."

"Presumably the ones that ain't dead."

"The rest of the guys that did Miami. The ones that didn't self-detonate."

"Right," I say, looking up at the drapes again. This time their pattern strikes me as more chaotic, less regular. "What did this note say?"

"It was short. Something along the lines of how disappointed they are that you're not an active participant in the task force."

"They're thinking these guys know you," Brady says. "Maybe worked with you in the program."

The program. That thing I've been trying to forget.

"And you're thinking I might remember who might have a thing for me." I give Brady a cold glare. "A long list, no doubt. You know how many guys I worked with, how hard I drove them. That leaves lots of candidates."

"Anyone in particular come to mind?" Dan asks.

I shrug. "May I see this note?"

Dan swallows again. "That's not necessary."

"Says bitter nasties about me, I take it?" Now I eye Taylor. "Something I would find *unsettling*?"

"They say they'll make sure you're involved next time they strike," Dan says.

"I guess they don't much care for blowing up my ranch, since I've given them plenty of opportunity over several days, and with TV coverage, no less."

"They would want to strike where they could cause maximum impact," Dan notes.

"Right. Lots of people. Me there. Throw in some military significance into it for extra credit. Maybe around the very seat of power." I look over at Brady, then at Dan. "How am I doing?"

"You got it."

"On top of everything else, they're gonna ruin my first marathon, ain't they?" I also think it, but don't say they're out to ruin my fancy prosthetic coming out party.

"We'll have full-on security," Brady says.

"Yeah, I'm sure you will. Just like at the Green Zone."

We don't say much after that. Brady and his team head out the door first, and I grab Dan by the arm before he can follow them.

"You doing OK?" I ask him.

He half smiles, half frowns, his way to point out this is the first time I ask him that. "Hanging in there, I guess."

"Lot of stress, I take it."

"A lot of responsibility." He pauses and something inside his eyes sharpens. "Good responsibility, though," he adds. "The kind that keeps you going."

I know where he's going with this. He

wants me to clue in that I too share that responsibility. He wants to pep-talk me into letting that responsibility keep me going. Keep me from giving up.

"Let me see that phone," I say.

He takes out his cellphone and unlocks it before he hands it over.

"There I am," I say.

"Told ya."

"Tight crop, though. Loses most of them nice trees in the background."

"It's not about the trees," he says at the moment I look up to catch his soft smile and the way his eyes are looking at me, offering me his soul.

I return the phone. "Guess not."

We stand there, both of us searching for what sort of physical gesture or well said words can communicate what we might feel for each other. In the end, we just say our goodbyes.

After Dan leaves, exhaustion sweeps over me. It's the kind that wallops you like a rogue wave, making you restless and not letting your body go to sleep. In my bed I use my tablet to watch the news over the Internet. I read up on the bombings, how air travel is being curtailed both because the government has mandated a reduction in flights after going to minimal crews to achieve fully trusted security at airports, and also because people are cancelling flight reservations.

Beyond the specific facts and event descriptions, I see more, though.

They're winning. They've scored a few points while we stumble and fumble. And regular, everyday people know it. Fear whips about like a tornado spout. Terror looms above us all in dark, heavy clouds that aim to reach down with fingers of destruction.

It's messy out there, much messier than in this body of mine, I tell myself. I should be thankful for what I have, even if someone snapped it into me without my consent. More than that, maybe what I have inside of me and those legs I wear can help clear this mess. Exactly how I don't know.

If Cassandra's right, purpose will show itself once I turn the corner.

I hear nails scratching at my bedroom door. Since I keep it open, it parts with more difficulty than I'd expect a big dog to have. But it ain't no big dog that comes in.

"Rover?" I ask in the darkness when I hear his rapid panting.

In the dim light of my night light I catch a glimpse of him in silhouette, standing next to me. My love and appreciation for all things canine notwithstanding, I'm not much for dogs sharing my bed. This time, though, I do not hesitate to slap the mattress next to me.

He's on my stomach in an instant.

I turn on my bed lamp so I can look into his eyes. There they are, brown and noble, full of understanding and love. In another second, I'm thinking back to how many times I looked into Shadow's eyes, how they looked like that on nights when after a gruesome day I needed to look into something pure and reassuring.

I almost cry at the thought, but Rover arrests my melancholy with a quick, furtive lick on the nose. Like a little girl, I giggle at him, and he takes that as invitation to further play and affection. I let him go until he tires himself out and lays at my side.

Someone at my side, I muse.

I turn off the light and think of Dan. I think of his last text to me telling me how fine I looked in my picture. I think about seeing my picture in his phone. That brings a smile to my lips, and a pleasant heaviness to my eyes.

Chapter 16

By the time two and half weeks pass and we fly out to DC for the marathon, no additional bombings have taken place. Some talking heads go on to claiming strengthened security measures at airports and the weeding out of personnel with questionable backgrounds have precluded additional attacks. Given what I know, it feels more like the eye of the storm.

And I'm that eye until someone yanks me into the outer bands.

All the same, three women and three dogs board a plane, a chartered one, thanks to the generosity of a prominent Wounded Warrior Project benefactor. He boards the plane with us, claiming he has some business to tend to in DC. I doubt that he has much business there, other than rubbing shoulders with a certain wounded warrior, but I welcome the gesture nonetheless.

By now Allison's marathon dream has crashed and burned. Her strained Achilles tendon won't budge, and she's been babying it for the past two weeks so she can preserve the ability to walk. She'll be our roving cheerleader, meeting us at a couple of points along the route, and taking care of Shadow and Shady when we're not running with them. Rover will stay with her for the duration of the race, doing his own kind of cheerleading.

As for Shady and Shadow, after some persuading by the powers that be, they will be running more than anticipated. I still won't allow a full marathon for them, but Cassandra has procured some running booties for them to help with strain on their paws. Over the past few weeks, we've had them train with them, and after some adjustments and adaptations, Shady and Shadow have taken to them well enough. That leaves us with a plan to run with them the first ten miles, and the last six. Why? Again, the folks in charge, Special Agent Dan

Murphy included, deem the start and end of the race as the most crowded spots, and hence, where our bombers might most likely strike.

The decision to run the dogs longer tickles Candice, my agent. She's angled hard about having them at the start line for photo ops with me and Cassandra. I resisted that idea, but now, my agent gets her wish. Social media bonanza coming right up.

When Sunday arrives, unlike most runners who ride the metro to the start line, we arrive at Arlington Cemetery aboard a black, government-issue SUV. Once there, two Marines escort Cassandra, the dogs and I to our corral.

Though the Marines usually hold their marathon on the last Sunday of October, ahead of Marine Corps birthday on November 10th, this year their new Commandant got a bright idea: since November 10th falls on a Sunday, let's run it then. According to Cassandra and Allison, this has raised a lot of dandruff in various running forums. In particular, talk about the cooler weather has bunched up more than one set of under garments.

Our running foursome takes the weather forecast as a good omen. We've trained in cooler Colorado weather over the past few weeks. Cassandra and I, and I'd like to think the dogs, too, welcome the crisp morning air with a smile.

"How are you feeling?" Cassandra asks, and she needs no further specificity.

She's noticed I'm still walking stiffly. Though nowhere near Allison's race-busting injury, over the last week or so, my body has also complained with the typical aches that come from pre-race training.

"Sore but OK," I say, slapping one of my hips.

"Back?" Cassandra asks.

"Not bothering me," I reply, leaving out the word "yet." If things go as they have the last two long runs, I'll have back pain on or about mile eight.

Cassandra leaves it at that, right at the time we approach a small group of reporters and photographers. For the next few minutes we, with Cassandra in the lead, answer a string of mundane questions about race prep, how we expect to do, and so on. I'm impressed. It seems for once we got us some kind reporters. They manage to avoid the elephant-in-the-room question until...

"There's been a lot of discussion about the Army announcement a few days ago," one of them says. "Do you think your prosthetic legs give you an edge over the other runners, Major McMurtry?"

"When you see me come in somewhere between five and six hours, I think you'll realize no one's giving me no winning medal, fancy legs or not. I'll also assure you that I much rather be running on the ones God gave me and some IED loon ripped away."

Cassandra leans in and adds, "What the major is saying is that her legs simply bring her up on par with the average runner. In other words, she has no unfair advantage."

She's done a great job smoothing out my reply, but I can't resist adding, "Now if someone flops me on a wheelchair and straps a rocket booster to its back, we might have something to talk about."

Laughter erupts among the reporters and a crowd of runners that's gathered around us. Shady lets out two quick barks, and before everyone takes that the wrong way, I'm smiling and rubbing her head to show she's nothing more than a normal, playful dog rather than a locked-and-loaded weapon.

After that we field a few more questions, and when I'm growing tired of it, I suggest we need to join one of the long lines over there by the portable latrines to let go of any extra burden we won't want to carry during the race.

As we approach the lines, I see that our Marine escort intends to take us to the head of the nearest line. I thank them for their thoughtfulness and insist we can stand in line like everyone else. I'm not sure if I did that to impress my fans or because I sense its rightness, or both of the above, but it gives us time away from the thick of the crowd, even if while standing there we get plenty of handshakes and "thank you for your service" greetings.

Back at the corral, now a few minutes before the start, Cassandra and I pick a spot on the side and toward the back to avoid getting in the way of faster runners, at least at the start. All the folks in this section are speedier than us, running in the 8 to 9 minute pace range, but our Marine escort doesn't want us too far back, which means their superiors and their superiors above them directed this placement. Though neither of us comments on it, Cassandra and I know why. They want us in the middle of the pack, at least toward the start of the race.

Up ahead, the national anthem plays. Saluting the faraway flag, I take a minute to think about all them graves to my left, the people in them, the families they left behind with a hope to return they could not fulfill. Tears roll down my cheek, and I don't care. Not even if some well-placed, clever photographer grabs a shot of it.

I came back, I tell myself. And here I am to run the race, the good race, as my preacher loves to say. I hope his words prove prophetic.

The music ends, the crowd claps, and

seconds later a Howitzer canon booms to signal the start of the race.

The first few steps come slow, scarcely above a walk to avoid tripping over the person in front of you. With each step, though, the congestion eases, and soon Cassandra and I reach our easy first mile target pace. We traverse the first mile in eleven minutes, and at the one mile marker, we raise our free hands, and we drop into a walk for the next minute, after which we resume the running.

At each mile marker, Cassandra uses her phone to check in and give Dan our location. He replies back each time with a brief "OK." We repeat this for seven miles, at which point we note how rather than continue to stretch out, the crowd begins to bunch up.

Cassandra has the course memorized, and she notes the National Mall lies ahead, on the way to the Capitol. "It's narrower there, so maybe that's it," she suggests.

Soon her suggestion's inaccuracy becomes apparent. At the point where we should restart our running, about one tenth of a mile into the eight mile, we come to a near standstill.

Before I can complain, Cassandra shows me the text she got from Dan. "Suspicious object found, mile 9. Bomb detected. Race stopped."

"Allison is standing somewhere around mile eight," I mutter.

Cassandra's voice wants to sound positive but shows strain nonetheless. "Yeah. She said she might meet us before, though, to walk with us for a bit."

"Yeah, maybe."

I look around. The runners behind us are beginning to crowd in. I'm beginning to feel trapped. We're all trapped.

"Cassandra," I say leaning in to her so that my lips nearly kiss her ear. "If you were going to detonate, where would you do it? At mile nine?"

She looks up at me, her face registering the fear welling up in me. "Here," she whispers.

Using my height I look around. I need a higher place. I find it. A few steps away I see a concrete cylinder that covers a trash receptacle.

"This way," I tell Cassandra.

We push through. When we get there, I hand her Shadow's leash and I climb on the trash can.

"Runners," I shout. "May I have your attention?" I repeat that three more times before I decide enough people are listening.

"I need you all to help me do something orderly and calmly." I repeat this again and add, "I need each of you to pass on the following message to all runners and then do it. Tell the person next to you, Major Jane McMurtry says to move away from the race course, calmly. Pass it on."

I see a few puzzled looks.

"Please do this. Tell the person next to you, Major Jane McMurtry says to move away from the race course, calmly. Pass it on." I point in the direction I want them to move.

A few start doing it, followed by a few more. Those close to me, already at the edge of the course, move toward a nearby street.

"Please do this," I repeat. "Tell the person next to you, Major Jane McMurtry says to move away from the race course, calmly. Pass it on."

More people comply. More start passing my message to their fellow runners. I look ahead toward mile nine, and see the sea of humanity parting before me.

I get down and tell Cassandra, "Let's go. Text Dan we're coming his way. Text Allison to get the hell off the course."

"Done and done," she says. "But do you think we should move ahead?"

"You mean because they're really after me? Because they're detonating around here?"

"Yeah."

I pat Shadow and point at Shady. "They'll let us know."

She nods and says, "Shady, *sook!*"

I say, "Shadow, *sook.*"

They both stand at attention, ready to move the instant Cassandra and I do. I breathe in, and we start trotting down the Mall.

The runners are thinning around us. My little trick worked, word spreading like a terror-fueled fire. I'm guessing whoever means us harm today is none too happy right now at the dissipation of intended targets when Shadow's taut leash snaps me out of my thoughts. I struggle to regain my balance and look back at Shadow.

"Not now!" I yell at him, seeing him there, chest and nose to the ground, rump in the air, frozen. Then I realize, no stupid Jane, now is the time. Exactly now.

"Cassandra!" I yell after her to see she too has stopped.

She's not looking back at me, though. Up ahead, a small woman is waving at us, her red hair whipping in the air. She's limping heavily and straining to hold on to a little dog that's pulling toward the inside of the race course. There a now abandoned water station stands as if pulled up in place by red, white and blue balloons. Helium balloons. Helium canisters, too, stand to the side, and I hope to God they're empty.

I look at Shadow, trace the line that his arrow-like snout paints, and see that it leads to that same water station.

"Allison, get off the course!" I yell back.

I wave at her. I point to my right.

"Allison!"

And then my world goes up in a bright, broad flash and a boom that shakes the earth far more convincingly than the Howitzer that started this good race of mine.

I go down on one knee, dragging Shadow to the ground with me, and the shockwave hits me flush in the chest like a leviathan's punch.

I don't know how much time passes. Right now there is no time.

Except for the ringing in my ears, the world has gone silent. I am sprawled like a discarded marionette on dirt and grass. Shadow sits next to me, calm in the face of it all. His blank face seems to say, "I've seen this and much worse. Not impressed. Bring it on."

Though I want to look after others, I know right now job one is to get myself together. More to the point, to reassemble myself. One of my legs feels lose, nearly detached, in fact. I shove it back in place and re-latch the fittings. For good measure I check and tighten the other. A moment later I'm getting up to my feet, swaying on my legs, facing toward the Capitol as the ringing in my ears gives way to emergency sirens. The ground beneath me shifts like the deck of a ship on rough seas.

My hips and back ache as I start trotting toward Cassandra. I find her on all fours, looking like she's about to start doing easy girl-style pushups. Though I almost call out her name, I know she can't hear me. I crouch and place my hand on her back.

She looks up, startled. And bleeding. I run my hand along the gash on her forehead. It's nothing but a scratch, I decide, and when I retrieve pieces of bark from her hair, I realize she scraped against the tree next to her, swept into it by the blast's shock wave.

I help her to her feet, and still woozy and wobbly, we survey the debris field. Only then do I ask myself, where is Shady? I look beyond, just on the edge of the crater, and there she is, standing by Allison. Or at least I hope that's Allison, not just a lump of what remains of her and Rover.

Cassandra and I stumble more than run as we strain toward the spot.

Shady cranes her neck upward and lets out one long moonless howl.

I take two steps toward Shady and Allison, but Cassandra pulls on my shirt and holds me back.

The sirens get closer, and Shady howls with them.

Chapter 17

"Thank you for giving us your statement," FBI Agent Zedinski says. He shows me his best duly mournful face. "You did good out there. If you hadn't—"

I raise my hand. "Got it. I'm a hero."

Dan steps in. "Give yourself a break, Jane. Thousands of people are alive because of what you did."

I close my eyes and rub the back of my neck. "With all of our brain power, we couldn't see that setup. We're so confident in our brawn. In our security. Jesus, Dan. They played us like a piano."

The room goes quiet. Though not much of a conference room, designed for doctors and other hospital staff to confer on how to save lives, it serves a different purpose now. With me as the guest of honor, taking up the head of the table, Brady and Taylor sit on either side of me. Taylor actually has her hand on my shoulder, how comforting of her, and I'm actually not slapping it away. Zedinski sits across from me, at the other end of the table, with Dan at his side. A small, sorry affair.

"We're going to get them," Zedinski says. "That area had tons of surveillance cameras. We're going to know who did it, especially as the runners and volunteers at the station cleared, it should become clear who belonged there, and who's acting a little strange."

I could point out all the missing slots in his logic and understanding, including how that thing could have been remotely detonated, or with a timer, with no one around to look weird or out of place right before the blast. But this ain't my job. I'm just the tracker, and no one's going to take what I say seriously.

"How's Cassandra?" I ask.

"A few scratches," Brady says. "They're doing a CT scan to check for concussion.

Banged her head pretty hard on a tree."

My lips break into a bitter smile.

"Listen, Jane," Dan says. "I know we've been over this, but are you sure you didn't see where that little guy went?"

By little guy he means Rover, and as I answer, I'm back in my bed, looking into his brown eyes, finding his soul, and letting him sooth mine.

"I told you. I saw him pulling away from Allison, toward the water station. Probably because he smelled the explosives. Then I looked at Shadow. When I looked back, all I remember is the flash of the blast. I don't even remember seeing Allison or how she—"

"OK, OK," Dan says in a soft voice.

But he soothes me none. "Like I told you, best guess is she let him go so she could move away, and he jumped right into the blast zone." I stop before I finish up with something crude, like I'm sure they'll find him in pieces up in what remains of nearby tree branches.

"It's still worth a check," Zedinski says.

"What check?" I ask.

He looks at Dan, and Dan takes over. "We were thinking you could help us, you know, track him. On the outside chance he ran away." He clears his throat. "He may have seen the bomber, recognized him, even. Maybe he went after him."

I'm about to object, but in fact, I have no basis. I've no idea how long I was down on the ground. Five to ten seconds is plenty for Rover to take off.

So, they want me to track him.

"Tell me about Allison," I say.

"She's in critical condition," Taylor says. "Doctors think she'll make it."

I stare at her, and I see it. The truth hiding under the truth.

"But?" I say.

Taylor shifts in her seat, looks down for a moment. "Doctors are also pretty sure she suffered irreversible spinal injuries. Still preliminary, but one of the best in the field examined her. She'll likely not walk out of here, possibly for life."

"Oh, she'll walk again," I say glaring at

Brady.

Taylor starts to say something, but she stops in mid-sentence.

Brady points at Dan, "He's not cleared."

"Dan?" I say. "Would you mind giving us some privacy?"

He frowns at me, holds my gaze for a few seconds, then gets up to go.

The door clicks shut, and I turn back on Brady.

"Allison will get very good care here," he says.

"Oh, the doctors here may be excellent. But Doctor Sven is way better, ain't he? And he's got better toys to play with. See where I'm going, *sir*?"

"It's not exactly subtle and nuanced."

"Glad I don't have to draw no pretty pictures. Allison's already briefed, signed papers and all. I'll talk to her myself. Believe me. She'll appreciate the advance notice, which is more than someone else got."

Brady stares me down, too, but I can tell he's not going to fight me on this. "I'll make the call, see what I can do."

"There's no trying, soldier," I say. "Just doing. Remember when you told me that?"

He grins. "I'll push it with all I got."

"She's going to Bethesda, tonight," I say. "And tomorrow morning Sven starts working on her. That's the kind of pushing you're talking about?"

His grin broadens. "Yes, ma'am."

The way he says that makes me wonder whether I'm doubling down on my deal with the Devil.

"We're a go then?" he asks.

"Not quite yet."

"Meaning?"

I lean back in my chair. "I require fuller insight before I put on my hip boots and wade into your swirling sewage."

"I'm not quite sure what you mean."

"Oh, but you do. Otherwise the FBI and Homeland Security would've come to do the beggin' and pleadin'. Instead it's you. And I'm thinking that might mean you have more skin in the game than love of God and country and a professional relationship with me."

"We can take Shadow and Shady from you. Have another handler lead the track."

"If you could, we wouldn't be having this nice conversation."

The muscles in his neck ripple as he swallows. "Alright. What do you need to know?"

"These guys, blowing themselves up for no good reason. It's more than blackmail of Iraqi nationals and PTSD-induced nuttiness, ain't it?"

"Such as?"

"Hmm. I'm thinking that if you can repair joints and nerve damage, that's only a scant millimeter away from tapping the mind itself."

Brady swallows again. "Go on."

I look over at Dr. Taylor. "I mean, if we want to repair those who are broken physically why not those who are broken mentally? Maybe they's broken both ways, so go for some of that wonderful synergy."

I pause to glare at Brady and Taylor. Looking at her, I add, "If we can put in a gadget that talks to nerves and augments bone, why not do one better and go for them precious neurons?" I turn to Brady. "How am I doing?"

Brady grins, looks over at Taylor. "I told you that for all her folksiness, she's some kind of crazy sharp."

I look down at the palm of my hand, scratched up from my trying to catch my fall during the blast. "This guy you want me to find. I'm guessing he's your prime case study. Among model patients, top of the class."

"Yes, ma'am," Brady says, and he's no longer grinning.

A cooling breeze ripples the green hospital scrubs I'm wearing over my running outfit. I stand at the edge of the crater holding two leashes in one hand, Shady and Shadow sitting on either side of me. As sunlight ebbs away, it all looks so different now. It's the light, I tell myself, all the while knowing that the primary responsibility for changing everything belongs to the explosion.

Blasts change everything. They blacken soil and whatever structures remain standing. They dig into the earth and toss it up in plumes of dust. They topple trees. They turn the hearing into the deaf. They carve into flesh and shatter bone. Most of all, they pound your soul to mush. They rob you of who you are, from the inside out.

"Ma'am," someone's saying behind me. "Here's the item you requested."

I turn to see a young man handing me Rover's small blanket-bed, back from the hotel already. Always nice when you can get good, prompt help.

I smell it first. I smell him as tears fight to run free. Bending down I let both dogs sniff it in unison. When I'm satisfied they got the scent, I hand back the blanket.

We start where we found Allison. "*Sook,*" I say, and they start tracking.

After a few seconds, they both look up and pull toward the nearby street, the one where the runners ran to.

"The runners," I whisper.

"What's that?" I hear Dan ask behind me.

I command the dogs to stop and half turn toward Dan. "The trigger man was a runner. Probably running right behind me, for all I know."

"How do you know that?" Dan asks.

"I don't know. I just do."

He tells one of the agents to check surveillance video for that, to look for Cassandra and me, then look behind us. "That should narrow it a bit. Anyone not peeling out but following them instead, he's our guy," Dan says.

Except he didn't, I don't say. Not if he blended in, stood behind a tree, tracked me from there, and pressed the button when he felt like it.

I hear radio squawking behind us, and I ask myself one more time if I'm ready to do this.

"OK, here's the deal," I say. "I lead, you guys follow. No one gets in front of the dogs unless there's a barrage of bullets coming our way and you want to be so gracious as to eat a few for us."

"Done," Dan says, he who should know that behind-the-dogs rule already.

"*Sook*!" I say, and off we go.

Both Shady and Shadow walk in tandem, resolute, without doubt. They got a solid scent, and one they should know well already. Their little buddy, let's go find him.

We walk down the Mall, in the direction of the Washington Memorial. I let them pull, and I trot behind them. I'm not about to slow them down, and hell, if I didn't get to finish my marathon, I might as well get in a mile or two now.

At 15th Street, we turn north, our pace quickening now with the urgency of a scent strong and pervasive. We come upon Pennsylvania. Having been here on more than one occasion, the emptiness of the streets and the flashing signals strike me with an eerie chill.

Shadow and Shady pause at the corner of Pennsylvania and 15th. I see the street is wet here. They've lost the scent, I fear. They look up at me as if imploring for guidance. For a brief moment I think to go left, toward the back of the White House, then look up 15th, catching a glimpse of the Old Ebbit Grill's sign. I figure either way we need to cross the street, so I do. On the sidewalk, Shadow picks up the scent first. Shady does likewise seconds later.

They pull me along toward the White House, across a park by one of the entrances. I came through here once during a visitor's tour. I stood for hours in line for it, and this time two dogs are saying I will get a fast pass.

"Anyone with us from the Secret Service?" I shout.

"Yes, ma'am," someone behind me says between labored breaths.

We stop at the gate, both dogs giving every indication they need to get through. From inside, a uniformed guard gives me and the two animals a weary look.

"We need access," I say. "Official business." I feel silly saying that as soon as the words leave my mouth, but heck, it's the truth.

The Secret Service agent steps up and shows his ID to the guard. "Stand by," he tells him, then turns to me. "Ma'am, are you positive?"

"One dog could be wrong," I say. "Two? As they say across the pond, not bloody likely."

Brady arrives at that point and spouts something well-worded about the reliability of these highly trained dogs. An FBI agent comes into the mix next, and soon an argument about jurisdiction and cooperation breaks out. I'm about to say something about how this is exactly why Congress can't get anything done, typical Washington, and a couple of other quips along them lines when another guard steps up and identifies himself as the supervisor on duty.

In a moment I'll never forget, he looks at no one else but me. "Ma'am, are you Jane McMurtry?"

"Yes, sir."

"Major Jane McMurtry?"

"She's the one."

"We got you on the list for tomorrow. Purple Heart ceremony, right?"

"That's correct, sir."

"Aren't you a little early?"

"No, sir. Actually I'm hoping I ain't late."

He takes that in for a second. "This about the bombing?"

"Yes, sir."

"What are you chasing?"

"A person of interest."

"You don't mean the bomber."

"I'm afraid I do."

He stares me down hard, and I'm preparing arguments along the lines of him not wanting a bomb to go off inside the people's house, when he says to his underling, "Open it up." To me he adds, "We'll go through protocol, then we let you do your thing. We'll be quick."

A second later we hear the gate's lock click open.

This time around I have no chance to enjoy the tour. I scarcely notice anything but that I'm going down corridors, up and down stairs, while a posse of Secret Service and FBI Agents blanket my six. The dogs slow and come to a door. Shady starts to whimper, and I shush her.

I point at the door knob, asking for silent permission to go in. Why? Square on the center of the door's top panel a red sign with white lettering says something to the effect that one can't enter this room without proper clearance. "No Piggy-backing," it reads in red letters.

One of the Secret Service agents comes up and turns the door knob for me. It's locked. Out of his pocket he takes out an access card, he waves it at a proximity reader, and a beep signals the door has unlocked. He starts to turn the knob, the door is starting to crack, when a single report sounds inside the office and before me and to the left of my face a bullet hole opens through the red sign. Splinters fly at my face.

I don't think. I do. Ducking and leaning in with all I got, I jam my shoulder into the door as I yell, *"Voraus, Fast. Voraus, Fast!"* I go in falling as I enter, and inside I see the tail ends of both Shady and Shadow disappear into a snarling darkness.

Another shot goes off, and I flinch, waiting for the shriek of a wounded dog. But I don't hear it. In its place I hear a man's voice scream in horrified pain, followed by the ripping of clothing and tissue, all wrapped in growling and more snarling.

Someone flips the light as I get up. We see him then, pinned against the wall, each arm held at the wrist by a dog's twisting jaw. Blood streaks the wall behind him in broad crimson brushstrokes.

I turn to the lead Secret Service agent. "May Special Agent Murphy and I have a minute, sir? It won't take long."

"Take all the time you want," he says, wiping a dribble of blood away from his cheek, I'm guessing from one of the splinters.

Dan steps in. "What are you doing?"

"You worry about what you're doing," I say. "Which is taking careful and thorough notes. Got something to write with?"

He gets out his cellphone. I turn back to Mr. Dog Meat.

"Major Arnold, is it?" I crouch to his right. "You dare come to my house and have me cook dinner for you, eat on my mother's china, and then you go off setting up nasty bombs? Now that's mighty rude of you, I think everyone would agree, especially these two."

"You can't do this," he says through gritted teeth.

"Why, I believe I'm doing it, so *can't* must not be the right verb. Now, we can worry about your diction and logic, or we can focus on more productive and painless things. Like you telling us who and where all your buddies are. Either that, or these two turn you into one big can of Alpo chunky meat."

"You can't do this," he repeats like it's going to work better this time.

"Honey, you have no idea what I and two pissed off dogs can do. Trust me when I tell you that's not an empty slot in your understanding that you would like me to fill in."

As if to punctuate my remark, Shadow gives a slight twist of his head. Major Arnold screams.

I steal a glance of something white to my right, and I see him. Rover, his neck twisted in an unnatural angle. Part of me wants to cry, part of me wants to kill, and the rest doesn't want to know the difference.

Chapter 18

They let me go outside, so I sit on the cold floor along one of the outside corridors, the cool of evening washing over me. They gave me a towel, too, in which I could wrap him and hold him against my chest. Shady sits at my right, Shadow at my left, both of them taking turns to sniff at me and at Rover. I cry. Audibly and not caring who hears. The three of us cry together, and occasionally Shady lets out one of her moonless howls.

Dan stands to my right, a few feet away, I'm guessing not a little uncomfortable at this show we're putting on in the house of the most powerful man in the world. But heck, they call it the people's house, and tonight one of the people and her dogs are in mourning. Because that's what people do. In any house.

"We got 'em all," he says for the third time. "We did good tonight, Jane. We got 'em."

Yeah, we got 'em, I think. And we lost our little hero.

I don't know how long our mourning goes on, but I suppose when the Secret Service declares all's secure, the big man decides he not only can but wants to move about. More than that, he decides he wants to see me and my dogs. He comes to us, nods at Dan, and approaches me and the dogs.

To his credit, he says nothing. He crouches down, places one hand on my shoulder and gives it a gentle, long squeeze. Next he pets Shady and Shadow, and last he places his hand on my hand, the one with which I'm covering Rover's eyes. He gives a soft squeeze there, too, shorter this time, and with that he gets up and walks away at a slow, unhurried pace, giving Dan a pat on the shoulder as he walks past him.

There it is, without words, and all that one needed to communicate. The way dogs do it. The way they say more than we try to conjure up with all our fancy, over-worked vocabulary.

This gesture settles me, and it has a similar effect on the dogs. I rise to my feet, and Dan comes over.

"Let's get out of here," I say.

"And him?" he asks about Rover.

"I suppose he can stay." I hand him the toweled bundle, and he sets it on a bench.

Together we walk out of the same gate where we came in. Outside a gaggle of press has formed. Cassandra meets me there, a white bandage around her head.

"Nice bandanna," I tell her with a forced smile.

She says nothing, taking the dog leashes from my hand.

The reporters start shouting questions my mind does not register. We walk a ways, doubling back by the Washington Memorial, making a left turn toward the Capitol along the National Mall.

"What are we doing?" Cassandra asks me.

"Yes, Jane," one of the reporter's parrots. "What are you doing?"

"I'm finishing my marathon," I tell them.

It takes Dan and Cassandra a few seconds to fully digest my meaning. I hear objections from Dan, none from Cassandra. I tell Dan to make himself useful, go get his car, buy us some water, and follow us along the route.

To Cassandra I say, "Still have the course memorized?"

"Yes, ma'am."

We arrive at the site of the explosion, have to go around it for all the yellow tape and police presence. Seconds later, with the gaggle of reporters giving chase, two women and two dogs start trotting. It doesn't take long for the reporters on foot to peel off, only to be replaced by those in cars and news vans, pointing spotlights and cameras at us. In my mind I'm picturing "LIVE" news coverage throughout the country covering the crazy big, ugly chick and her three sidekicks running a blown marathon.

A few locals catch on and come out to run alongside us a few blocks at a time. Some stick with us longer. Soon about twenty or so of them follow us, some carrying and waving flags, hollering and hooting it up for the cameras and for us, I suppose.

"We're making some serious buzz now, ain't we Cassandra?"

She grins at me, and we keep running.

A few miles later she says, "I hope this is not some precursor to you skipping out on the Purple Heart ceremony tomorrow."

"Only God knows, right? Did I ever tell you the first guy that ran a marathon died?"

She grins at that, too, and we quicken our pace.

It hurts to run. We manage it by walking when we feel like it. One step after another, stride after stride, we push on. We don't feel good or glorious, just pain. I think about all the other pain I carry inside me, the non-physical kind. It occurs to me that you can hide pain inside pain, too, and that's the best you can hope   for.

Staying in Touch

I hope you have enjoyed reading this story as much as I enjoyed writing it. If you would like to stay in touch with me and learn about future releases, join my reader's club at http://eduardosuastegui.com. From time to time, my newsletter will contain free downloads that I make available to my readers.

You may also send me an email with comments and feedback about this and other books at eswriting@gmail.com, or through my social media channels:

Twitter: http://twitter.com/eduardoauthor

Google+:

http://plus.google.com/+EdSuastegui

You can learn more about writing at http://eduardosuastegui.com. Once there, I hope you browse through information about the *Our Cyber World* and *Tracking Jane* series.

Our Cyber World...
where cyber technology, artificial intelligence,
espionage, and electronic surveillance intersect.

Stories in this series…

Dead Beef

Pink Ballerina

Active Shooter

Decisive Moment

Beisbol Libre

Ghost Writer

Random Origins**

Feral**

Semi*

DroNET*

Recombinant**

* Free when you join my mail list

** In work, to be released soon

Meet Major Jane McMurtry.
Her voice will draw you into her pain.
Her struggle will show you how to overcome.
In her search for love you will find hope.

Stories in this series…

Waiting for Shadow

Shadow-7

Rover

Fleeting Shadow *

Tahoe-1

Brownie

Blood Track

*Heart Track***

* Free when you join my mail list

** In work, to be released soon

Eduardo Suastegui

http://eduardosuastegui.com

Made in the USA
Coppell, TX
31 May 2022

78278168R30149